Predetermine

MIRANDA GUYER

Trafford rev. 08/21/2015

North America & international
toll-free: 1 888 232 4444 (USA & Canada)
fax: 812 355 4082

I would like to take this page to dedicate to the people that have encouraged me to follow through with the book. I thank my mom, Valerie, giving me her full support in the matter as well as my brother, Will, for introducing me to Trafford. Thank you to my friends, Dominique, Aleah, Tonteonna, Kayla, Sammi, and Alex for also the support and read overs. I could not do anything of this without any of them. Also for the people who have taken the time to help me when I needed it. I hope also to any of my readers who enjoy reading the book as much as I did when writing it. As I said I hope to further the writing world with my own stories and create a new spark in the reading world.

Chapter 1

My mother gently brushed my long hair that went down to the middle of my back stroke by stroke as I sat on her comfortable bed. My hair was long enough at the time I could have reached behind and tug on it without stretching my arm. I loved when she brushed my hair, it felt so nice. Sometimes when I couldn't sleep she would brush it, that always did the trick to have me out in minutes or it was the fact my head was resting on her lap for comfort. I was not really sure what actually did the trick.

Mom always said to have my hair up high so nothing happened like it getting dirty, as if that helped for me. She suddenly stopped brushing, realizing she had to get something for today, then got up. I felt betrayed because she knows I didn't want her to stop as she knew, as well as I did, she could have continued on forever. Before she left the room she turned and looked at me. It seemed she had been quietly sobbing behind me and I did not hear one sniffle or feel one tear.

I wondered what she was doing exactly. I heard her go toward my room, open the closet door, and shuffle around. She returned with clothing grasped in her right hand and I realized I was still in my pajamas. They were of my favorite sports team in baseball, which everyone puts down for the count. I always told people to give them a chance and they'll win, but they would usually find something to say in return. In the end they would shut up thanks to my witty comeback. For a thirteen year old, I had a smart mouth that I was always told to watch as it was going to get me in trouble. Anyway, in her trembling hands were a gray long sleeve sweater with black silky dress pants and in her right hand were a pair of black flats with tiny sparkles. I never liked to wear those kind of shoes. They were uncomfortable and my feet would always flip out, literally. I could hit someone in the face with the precise flip. All of that was part of my collection of nice clothes, meaning that I did have dresses. I prefer my clothes with legs and not like a wrap that sometimes makes you walk like a mermaid. The only time I ever wore nice apparel was at certain special events that required this type of dress. This was one of these days; I was about to have my life planned out for me.

It was only about a week ago from this time when my parents got the notice of my, what is called, Predetermine. In this country of the world each state in its capital has four members at a time decide the fate for each child when they turn the age of thirteen. From what I remember from my schooling it has been around almost one hundred years. It began after the war when crime and violence rates went up because their weren't enough jobs for returning soliders and the government only cared about their own paychecks. I was told it kept the people in line and the balance of the world so another break out doesn't occur. Every place has a different way in keeping this balance. Some others have the Predetermine while others just flat out have cruel justice systems. The cruel systems where you do one little violation and everything goes to hell. The whole good and evil mambo jumbo; it is a perfect world. Everyone must go through it, not matter what or who you were in society. You could almost say it is a combination and a battle of conformity and individuality. Not being allowed to live your own life the way you choose to instead following the guidelines set by someone who does not even know you. The worst part of this was that one week ago was my thirteenth birthday.

To finish up getting me ready my mother curled my hair and placed it up in a ponytail with hair still coming out down my back. Morely described as a half up and half down appeal. I didn't mind that hairdo, unless she had left it all the way down. It was beautiful, just not my style. She also put my bangs off to side and placed some on my head with bobby pins. Every time she looked at her work she said it looked nice, but I disagree because I am more of a tomboy. I like my jeans with holes tore in the knees and t-shirts that had deep green grass stained in them that do not come out. Well I guess I should count my blessing I get to wear dress pants and not a dress.

Not everyone gets a good Predetermine and my parents were lucky. My mother's Predetermine was to marry, have two kids, and be a social worker. Not really what she called as her ideal life except the marring and kids. Her name was Kenari Siyas and her maiden name being Reigus. She met my father in school and his name was Arrington Siyas. He was also to have two kids, marry, and be a landscaper. He didn't mind that he had that for a job. He could always draw and then take the drawing to create the most beautiful of structures and areas for the people. This was a way he could make the drawings into reality for people to enjoy to stare at for hours. Looking at the designs was nicer to view than watching paint dry, but with his paintings you actually could sit there and watch it dry. Whenever mom could not find she would always know I was out in his workshop being in a trance at the ideas that came out of his creative mind. He actually did most of our house, the small pond in the front yard and the garden with colors inside and out. This was why I had enjoyed coming home every day to this beautiful scenery. Because they knew each other it didn't seem like an arranged marriage as most did.

Our country only had one law; **DO NOT** break the Predetermine that you are given. The main question was what would happen if someone did? Before you receive your actual one they teach in school what it is all about to prepare you. It seemed more like a way to scare poor children and give them nightmares. I remember coming home traumatized by what we were told and hung on for dear life to my parents wondering if it was true. Sadly, I was told the truth and as long as I behaved I would be safe. How could anyone do that to a human being? The main question that me and my class asked was, what were the consequences for breaking your Predetermine?

Well, far out in our country about 1,000 miles away far from civilization were prisons or what people who behave call behavioral prisons. They were designed to straighten law breakers out. They were cruel and unjust to anyone; no matter the age unless under thirteen. If under the age they could not place a hand on you unless you actually committed a crime. You could be as young as thirteen and they would not care. You broke their laws and someone had to pay the price

The tool used in the prisons to put sense into people was hard labor or what seemed torture, whichever came first. Anyone who worked there or in the government believed that it would put justice into people not to break their Predetermine again. They never saw the cruelty. It depends on which part of the Predetermine you broke decided how long you would stay trapped and then released. People went in, but some, they never came out or were seen again. If they did it would be a cry in the wind.

I had about two hours before my Predetermine was called upon so my mother told me I could take my younger brother, Vaughan, outside to play, as long as I was careful not get dirty, like that would happen. Me . . . not getting dirty, was a wish for mother. When I walked outside onto the porch I only breathed the cool air for a second before my hand was pulled to the yard. I took my shoes off because it was difficult to run and I had rather not risk tripping. My mother would rather have dirty feet than me trip and have dirt and grass stains on my clothes. We chased each other, playing all our mini games. We created these to keep ourselves entertained either out or inside. They varied form playing as explorers, animals, or acting as our favorite characters from our favorite shows. As I turned to return the chase I saw my best friend Atticus and his little sister, Bethany, walking toward us. Atticus and I have known each other since the age of seven when we started the second grade. He lived just down the road from me.

"Hey," he said. In his voice I could see he was upset about something.

"Hey to yourself," I answered. I didn't mean to, but it was in the same tone as his, "Are you okay?"

"I don't want to talk about," he answered. He nudged Bethany to play with Vaughan; he knew where this was going and didn't want her to hear the words that could roll off his tongue.

"You can tell me anything," I said grabbing my shoes and sitting on the porch. I gestured him to come and sit with me and my eyes began to tell him to spill or else.

"I know that it's not like me, but I'm scared about my Predetermine today," he confessed with his head down giving into the non-existent threat.

I was shocked by his words in more ways to think. This was my fearless friend who beat up kids in the second grade when they put my face in the dirt after I got in a fight with them over picking on Vaughan. This was when we had first met. I knew I was too young to get in a fight, but that was my little brother who was just starting the first grade. The other thing was that he didn't tell me that his Predetermine was that day. His birthday was a week before mine. I couldn't believe I had forgotten about the Predetermine system. All of them are done at the end of a child's birth month.

"I didn't know," I said being as sorry as possible. I was sorry as I felt blind for not noticing sooner. I wanted to face palm myself, but I knew that would start Atticus on a lecture about I shouldn't be feeling guilty.

"I know that too. Only my family knew about today. I'm sorry that I didn't tell you about it. In fact, I didn't want you to know," he said.

That was odd to hear him say. Atticus told me everything and I did too. Why not this? Was it not important enough? I saw it was. His life was about to be planned and it had the chance of me not being in it. What was he worried about? I respected him by not asking. It had to be his choice whether or not to tell me.

"It's going to be fine! Trust me!" I said collapsing his hands with mine. I smiled with eyes closed which was a habit I picked up from being with my dad so much. I always missed something when I did. All I was doing was to put some cheer into this depressing situation. As I said I miss imprtant details with my eyes closed as I never did see Atticus's mad blush. When I finally opened them he stopped, but I still could see a small amount of red remaining in his cheeks.

"Thanks," he said. I usually had the right or wrong thing to say, never in between. This time was right.

"Mallca!" I heard my mother shout my name. Then she noticed me on the porch or the fact my hands were still holding Atticus's.

"Oh, well it's time to go dear. Atticus, your mother called and said that it was time to go."

We looked at each other and sighed. Time was something I learned quickly that passed too fast. I can be busy with one activity until the time for something else and next I know it is time for whatever something else was. What did our moms do with this remaining time? They checked to see if we were dirty. I had to go in quickly to wash my feet. Other than that I passed my inspection then we were to our cars and were on our way to what awaited in our lives.

I sat in the back of our car with Vaughan beside me. It was quiet ride. Our usual car rides were never silent. We always had some topic to talk about, either weird or normal. A normal conversation was a rare conversation in my family. Every once in a while I caught Vaughan glancing over at me.

"What?" I finally asked after like the tenth time he looked in five minutes.

"It's nothing," he answered. I gave my look when I know something is up and I want to know what it is. Actually I almost gave Atticus the same look earlier. That was why he told me willing. I had used it so many times he figured no one can hide anything from me. Sometimes all I had to do was narrow my eyes and glare like I was reaching into their soul. "I hate when you do that!"

He-he, I had broken him and less than a minute too, that was a new record for both of us, me breaking him and him giving in.

"I know," I said proud of this achievement, ". . . so what's wrong?"

I could see he thought about not telling me again, but he should know better by now. Out of all the people I have known in my life he has gotten the look the most. The people to get it the least was my parents because that is unstable grounds I had rather not cross.

"Okay . . . I'm worried about your Predetermine today," he confessed.

"I know that, we all are. It will be fine." I answered in some way repeating from earlier today. I realized that this a time when people are uneasy.

"How do you know? You seem so calm," he answered.

"I'll let you in on something. I don't have a clue and just like you so I'm worried too. I know for the family I need to stay tough and calm," I explained in a voice of pride. Vaughan looked like he was going to cry.

"I love you Mallca," he said. It was a nice moment between us until my brother added, "even if you turn out to be a murderer or a homeless person."

Thanks Vaughan, the nice moment between us was ruined. I bet it would be a while before the next one and knowing him, he'll ruin that one too. When I looked forward I saw my mom staring back at me, she had heard every word. I smiled and she returned the gesture. She didn't have to tell me that she proud of me.

Almost the entire trip I wondered what I would get for a Predetermine; I hoped not a murderer or homeless person. Was it going to be acceptable or terrible? As I said to Vaughan I was worried, but whatever my Predetermine was I had to take it or be taken away.

Atticus had the same kind of thoughts in his mind. His included:

Will ours affect our friendship?
Will Mallca's Predetermine be close to mine?

With all my years of knowing Atticus Joseph Issigna, my best ~~friend~~, had a crush on me. I have to give credit where credit is needed because he did a pretty good hiding his feelings from my sights. I wondered when this all started. Was it the day he saved me from the bullies and became my friend or afterward? I questioned his choice of girl, who would fall for me, Mallca Azria Siyas? Known as the girl who is the contentious tomboy, and not afraid to get dirt on a dress with shorts underneath.

To be honest when I looked at him, saw him, and his personality I felt different then I had before. His hair was short and brown, but not too short as if it were a military cut. His eyes were blue like the sky on a darker, good, blue day. He was about four inches taller than me and was athletic looking, more than me at least. I knew eventually he was going to be like six feet based on how tall his dad was. He had a height of six foot four. His voice wasn't deep, but he sounded like a guy. Putting it all together he was cute and I saw why the girls at my school agreed. They told me I was lucky to be known as his best friend when they could barely even talk to him. I made it seem so easy, well I had known him for years. I knew what I saw in him, but what was his excuse? My excuse was I was thirteen and just starting seeing boys in a new light.

As I said I have long hair at about my middle of my back and it was dark brown that could match tree bark. It was always up in some way except pigtails. My eyes were dark brown, with light brown flecks, and that seem to blend with my black pupils. People say they look like the color of dark chocolate, which I hate. I was indeed short in height, or at least I think five foot three is short, but average for a girl my age. Along with my height I was built not skinny athletic, but more like a catcher in baseball. Never really thought of myself as beautiful or pretty, but people said I was. My little amount of friends and family told me that, but I think it is because they have to. All that time thinking about Atticus started to make me think of him more than my best friend.

Twenty minutes later we had arrived and I slowly removed myself from the car. I actually think if I could I would bury my fingernails into the cushion of the seat. Looking across the lot I saw Atticus in black dress pants with a white shirt tucked in and a black tie. I knew his mother tied it because I knew he couldn't.

He was looking sharp for my best friend.

I waved my hand only once as a sign of hello and good luck. I don't think he saw me as he didn't return it. As we walked in I saw other children my age. The entire time thoughts of how this would turn out rolled in and out. I could never get them to stop and I was about to lose my sanity.

Out of a room came a mother balling her eyes out and a father that looked as if he was going to cry. The boy looked shocked and lost for words. Someone had just signed his death certificate. At his mother's side was his little sister, who looked only seven, confused on what was going on. Now my nervousness started transforming into fear and became worse with each passing minute, no second. I turned and wanted to run away, but I ran into my father's chest.

"It's okay," he said trying to calm my fear gripping me by my shoulders in attempt to keep me from running away. He also told to face my fears and not run away from them.

"I'm scared," I told him in a crying voice.

"I know," he said, "and I'm going to be right here for you."

"Mallca, its time," my mother said interrupting our father daughter talk. Thanks mom, the sarcastic part of me wanted to say. She came and touched my shoulder that if I didn't have control would be shaking. I thank my dad for that.

We walked in the room that seemed like a dark courtroom. Actually this whole place seemed like a courthouse. With what this entire deal meant I could see why. The room only had ten chairs. Four were behind stands sitting tall behind a long table. Three sat in front with the middle sticking out more in front. That chair was for the one being predetermined.

Why did that day have to be me?

"We shall now being the Predetermine of Mallca Azria Siyas,"

said a voice of the three that were in the room. With that a tall black haired man came in and sat in the empty chair next to the four. I wondered why my Predetermine have five instead of four. I later knew he was just observing. My parents recognized him the "dictator" of our area or known by name as Terreagan Illingsworth. My parents were bewildered at what would he be doing at their child's Predetermine. It was a rare sight and most people thought of this as an honor. I didn't think so.

These Predetermines were usually quick to the point meaning no fluffy business. I learned this when I saw my first Predetermine, as an observer. Before a thirteen year old receives their own Predetermine they first observe another's. That was the reason for the three chairs in the back of them room.

I felt sorry for the girl who I had to watch about this time last year. She was to have four kids and one before the age of eighteen. Also she would marry a bad guy and be an artist. This guy would be the father of the last two children and would not be any help. I could not have the kids because I don't care for them unlike Atticus. The guy she had to live with the rest of her life would drive me over the edge and I would break my Predetermine to murder him for being a douche. Being an artist would be the only part I could have lived with.

Atticus told me about the boy he had to watch only about a day after me. His wasn't good either. First getting caught up with the wrong crowds, then to be douche bag himself. In the end he would get his life together and succeed. Well, the first part sounds bad then turns good. I guess there is hope for a good Predetermine after all. My parents worried that I could turn up like the children they have had to watch all these years.

I was scared.

I was scared for Atticus, my family, and myself. People who I was scared for kept rushing in my head until a loud judgmental voice roared across the room causing silence. It was funny that the room was already quiet.

"You have been decided! I shall begin," said the older man on the far right side with white hair and who looked like he had a stick up his...I think you get it. If not, I was going to say butt, sure, let's go with that. I closed my eyes, praying, hoping, breathing, if I remembered to, that whatever it was could be acceptable. Each person of the committee would say a part of my Predetermine. It seemed like forever to get on with it. The suspense was killing me.

"You shall marry . . ."

Dammit. Marriage was something I never looked forward to because sometimes you aren't able to pick. Yes, I knew for a thirteen year old, at the time, I had a smart mouth. My parents were proud...that they didn't know.

"In sometime of your life you will become of a serious illness . . ."

Double damn, but he didn't say I would die . . . yet.

"Have no children . . ."

I could live with that. At least they wouldn't suffer through this as I do.

"Your job is to be an archeologist . . ."

Then I really whined inside.

That kind of subject of history puts me to sleep. The past is the past and should be left there until a later date that doesn't concern me. Seriously, it is dead, ever heard of leave the dead alone. Partly it was I could never get into enjoying that subject. To be honest it wasn't as bad as I had thought it could come out to.

"I see you will also be trouble and be my Breaker . . ." Illingsworth said in a hushed voice. I read his lips and even heard what he had said, but just barely. Also, I think I was the only one who did hear him.

"Daughter of Arrington and Kenari Siyas, Mallca, you have been predetermined!"

Of course I got the speech about living by my Predetermine and such or face the consequences. I had heard it all before and nothing was new, except the people telling the story. That did not make it any more interesting and even then I was about fall asleep from hearing it at school. And again I didn't care as I get it.

Having to seem like I was paying attention was more difficult than I had believed. To keep my mind at work I focused on a painting on the back wall of the room. It was of . . . well I'm not sure actually. The picture was of a cross and a hammer. I did not know what could that have meant? Then I got it.

It's a picture that represents of government, the law, and religion. A person lives by the Predetermine given by what is believed by the hand of someone greater through others. People like the determiners believed that to be them. I was snapped out of my concentration by the slam of a hammer on wood; it was finally finished and set in stone.

As we all left the room I noticed that Atticus was no longer waiting outside with the other children that had their own Predetermines today. It only meant one thing; he was next.

"Atticus Joseph Issigna, you are determined!" He as well hoped for the best.

"You shall marry."
"Have no children..."
"You may or may not lose your spouse."
"And you shall become a doctor."

"Son of Daphnia Issigna and Father of the deceased, Atticus, you are predetermined!"

This was going to interesting to see how it all played out.

My parents seemed fine with how today's events occurred or at least the best as they could. They were pleased at the Predetermine except about me getting sick and possibly dying. Which I wasn't sure how that was even going to happen. Did they expect it to happen magically or on the job? Atticus's mother only had bad feeling that he may lose his spouse as she did. At least he wasn't the one who had to die in the end.

Today during my Predetermine I noticed something I wished I hadn't until the day when his did arrive. My twelve year old brother was watching my life unfold. This only meant one thing; his Predetermine was inching closer.

You would figure since Atticus and I told each other everything we would be at each other wanting to know how each other's had gone. Well . . . that was not the case. We didn't speak to each other all day or let alone the entire week. I tried to talk with him at every chance, at school, seeing him in the neighborhood, but he would not even acknowledge me. Not even a simple hello or a wave. Bethany could not get him to even talk to me and she didn't know why either.

On Saturday my parents just needed to relax and going out seemed likes the best way to handle it or to get away from the main subject of the chaos in the week. My mother even invited Daphnia to tag along. At first she was reluctant about the idea, but my mother said just to bring the kids here. It was a shock when my mother told me what she had done. It was going to be weird since Atticus did not really speak to me. I was both in a good mood and wanted to kill her.

While our parents were out doing whatever they did, Vaughan and Bethany played with anything to keep them entertained. They played anything from videogames to board games. I never babysat anyone because I never know what to do to keep kids out of trouble. Also the fact Vaughan and I are so close in age if would not have matter. Atticus and I sat quietly in the living room. I could hear the clock tick with every tock like I was taking a test and he knew my score. I didn't know how to start a conversation that wasn't stupid and it was killing me not talking to him. I was almost tempted to just go to sleep.

"So are we partners for the street hockey tournament next month as we usually are?" I asked. For as long as I remembered since we learned hockey, my area had two on two competitions for entertainment each year around this time. Children can enter as young as eight to fourteen and Atticus had always been my partner or people called "my partner in crime." We won the first year we competed too and every year afterwards.

I remembered being tied at two with only a minute to go in overtime. Of course this is street so it wasn't as exciting as a true ice hockey match. Atticus had the ball or puck which ever you may call it and I was on the other end. You may think you need three, one to be goalie, but nope. When you're on offence you have none, but one soon switches to defense and runs down to guard. Anyway it was like a movie with Atticus passing the puck between the guy's legs and me shooting it with enough force to make the other fall and the puck go in. I loved those times, even when I do not admit it.

"I don't know," he muttered quietly. This silent treatment was getting old and I had enough. He was not himself and was made clear that something was on his mind.

"That's it! I can't take it anymore!" I said raising my voice standing above him.

"Take what?" he questioned nervously at my sudden outburst. Did I have to spell it out? "Do not play dumb with me," I snapped.

"I have to make sure we are on the same page," he replied being cute. I admit it was cute and funny, but it was so not the time. Plus, it was not fair as used that line on him once. I thought 'he thinks I'm crazy', and that would not be the first time.

"You haven't talked to me all week and it starting to worry me," I confessed, and then it hit me. I felt so dumb not thinking this before. What had just happened to us? "Is it the Predetermine?" I had asked in a softer tone to escape the yelling.

He nodded.

"What happened?" I asked sitting next to him.

"I'm scared about us," he said quietly.

What does he mean by that, us?

Last time I checked that word is used when two people are in a relationship and are dating. I am pretty sure that is not the case here.

"Did they say anything about us not being friends?" I said implying that I am his friend no matter what.

"No, nothing like that," he answered.

"Then what is it?" I asked.

What could be so bad that makes him not want to talk to me? Reject your best friend?

I noticed that I was asking too many questions and it would stop if he gave real answers. Maybe I should stop so I could get them?

"I'm worried about that our Predetermines will affect us. To be honest, I don't want anything to change," he admitted.

I got my answer and wished I hadn't. I didn't know how to respond to that comment. What could I say? That it doesn't matter because I won't let it.

"Oh," I started then it came to me, make him at least smile and bring it up as I want to talk about it, "I may bore myself to death with my job."

I got what I wanted. Atticus smiled and gave a small laugh at my comment. He knew all too well what field my job was under. I would be the only person to die from being bored.

"I see. Well I have to deal with injured and sick people," he answered. "You'll die of boredom and I'll die of an illness."

I knew what he got. He was to be a doctor. Now that I actually think about this situation; they switched jobs on us. The field of medicine has been my interest while objects in history fascinated him. Those bastards, I had to know more of what he had been destined to live by.

"What else?" I asked curiously.

"Well apparently I marry and want kids but never have them. It must be my wife's Predetermine," he answered.

Triple damn. It was all like me, but I couldn't just leave the boy hanging.

"Me too, except I don't want them," I said.

"Speaking of wife, mine may or may not die," he added completing his Predetermine.

How many times did I think damn to myself that day?

Counting the, *quadruple damn*, I've got four from that day in total.

Atticus's and my Predetermine matched perfectly to each other. I didn't tell him about me getting sick then he might notice the similarities too. We looked at each other with searching eyes and I saw that we could be each other's Predetermine.

Chapter

2

A tticus and I hardly spoke about what happened that night with our Predetermines. Neither of us, mainly me, didn't want bring it up as a topic of discussion in a conversation, but that did not mean I didn't think about it. It also was helped always avoiding the subject being brought up. Just say something else that sparks when he gets the look of about wanting to talk about it. That usually does the job. This topic is more like an Atticus wants to talk about then I'll have my topic. It seemed like everything was back to normal, almost. It didn't matter how much I tried I could not shake the thoughts of the match-up. Also the fact it doesn't end well for either of us because I could probably end up dying and Atticus loses his best friend and possible spouse. Questions still kept popping into my head like popcorn in a microwave with so many coming at once before having the time to actually think about the answer to each one.

Was that just a common decision that was made for people that oddly went with someone else's?

Is Atticus the guy for me?

Right now keeping secrets from him is a pain because that's not the only thing I hiding, actually I haven't told anyone anything. Only myself knew about what I saw Illingsworth say to me in the room. I think at the moment it should be the least of my worries. It is the rest of my Predetermine that has my hair standing.

Speaking of Predetermines making hair stand, it was about my younger brother. Vaughan is one year and three months younger than me. I was born in August, the fifthteenth to be exact, and his birthday was in November on the twelfh of the next year. It's a deal of for three months I am two years ahead of him and when November comes it is only by one. Time is an unexplainable concept when it comes to how it moves along. It either moves fast or slow. In this case it has gone by too fast.

The day was now in November and it was Vaughan's birthday of next year. I was already fourteen, living with my Predetermine for a year already, and Vaughan just was thirteen. It would be any day that his time would come. It was not the time to think about that when we had a party with family and friends with fun and games. Oh, can't forget the cake and ice cream too. It wouldn't be a birthday party without it. The only family that lived close was my aunt and uncle and their kids. In addition the only friends that could come were Atticus and Bethany. Of course their mother came, so that helped with the size. So by number of people it doesn't seem like much of a party, but usually the less people there leads to having more fun.

The party started at one o'clock and was until three, but who can put a time on a party. It ends when it ends. Usually goes until four-thirty knowing my family. Games were a big part until gifts which lead straight into cake and ice cream. However, a mailman happened to show during this time.

I know, what could be exciting about the mail? The only reason mail could be interesting is when something arrives with your name on it or you're expecting a package or letter. Most mail is junk or in parent's case, the bills which everyone just wants to throw out into the trash or what my family calls file thirteen.

Today the mailman didn't put the mail into the box out front, but handed it directly to my father. I had seen something like this a year and three months ago which was the day I turned thirteen in August. A Predetermine date has been decided and Vaughan's had just arrived.

I could see some of the mailman's Predetermine just by looking at him and what he was doing now. Bring people the worry of life only by delivering a letter with a message that never changes and has a date. This letter enclosed the rest of people's lives. By the guy facials, body language, and eyes he doesn't seem to be enjoying his job either. I don't think anyone would want the job where "don't shoot the messenger", actually comes into play.

My father looked at the letter with the eyes of that the envelope contained test results telling him whether or not he was going to live or die. Well, they kind of were, just for my brother. I wanted to tear the letter to shreds leaving it their like the dead that deserved to die. Slowly he opened the envelope and slid out the letter. I could clearly see his head and eyes move reading the letter over carefully.

After he finished his eyes looked shot and he handed it to my eager mother. She didn't take the time to read it knowing what it already said. Placing it on the table, both her and my father walked over to my bewildered brother. Embracing him tight and I think I can see them crying. When no one was looking I sneaked over and read the letter:

Dear Mr. and Mrs. Siyas

    The day has arrived for your son, Vaughan Siyas, to have his Predetermine. The date is set for November twenty-forth. All family in the household should be in attendance. If no one is to show on November twenty-forth, we can guarantee their will be consequences shall be given to the entire family.

                The Committee

I had a foul taste in my mouth. I wasn't sure if it was the mood that made the sweet cake taste that way or was it just the mood itself. With the date on replay in my head I began to think about it. It was at the end of next week. My little brother was about to loss having a free life, as I once did, to living by guidelines to the letter. Now my only hope for his sake was it wasn't anything sinister or in trouble.

A couple days later I sat in the almost complete darkness, with only a lamp on, that night I just feeling melancholy. Nodding off and falling asleep was a good idea as my eyes just kept dropping and opening. I was seconds from falling asleep when a knock occurred at my door. It was Vaughan and apparently he needed to talk to his older sister.

"Mallca, can I ask you a question?" he asked just sticking his head in the door to make eye contact with my droopy pair.

"Yeah sure," I replied, "Was that your question?"

Whenever I get the chance I take it to a joke. It took Vaughan a couple seconds to understand, he sometimes can be dense.

"Your funny," he answered noticing my joke and replying sarcastically. Usually I'd tell him that sarcasm was my job, but I let it slide. I am amused by this and everyone knows it.

'Smartass' was the thought both of us had.

"What was your question?" I ask being serious now that I have regained my composure.

"What was the Predetermine like?" he asked taking breath and coming straight out without any extra talk. I hate when people beat around the bush. If you have something to tell or ask me then do it.

I didn't know how to answer that question. I think it's a sick joke to the committee, but I couldn't tell him that. He wanted support and telling him that would scare him into not wanting to get it, meaning you get the same consequences if you broke it. Mine put me on my toes and felt like I was not too young to have a heart attack. Just be honest, not too honest though.

"Well, I thought it was scary to see what they would give me and if it could be bad or not. Just promise me that you will follow it and never break it. I need to make sure nothing is going to happen to you," I explained grabbing his shoulders and looking into his eyes. He had to know I was serious and this isn't one of the games we play.

"Okay," He nodded.

It was just like the time when I was going to my own Predetermine and we just talked. He has always tried to be the tough guy of the family and we all can see right through it. Even though he didn't look like it I could tell he was as scared as I was. Maybe it is a brother sister connection or it is that obviously seen in his body language and eyes. I'm glad he came to me about this instead of mom and dad. Knowing my parents and their role as parents, to protect your children, they would have told him a flat lie. When he figured it out they did it he would have not been nice as his temper peeked. At least my answer gave him clarity and yes, in a way, I did also lie to him. He knows better not to mess with me.

In truth I was terrified inside and out, but did not show it. It feels like jumping out of your own skin and run away until you're caught. Just even thinking about it makes my knees shake. The way each person spoke to you, like a chilling breeze that runs up your spine. People say I was lucky enough to walk away with what I got. If anything happens to Vaughan he can live with me and my husband, no matter the rules, which at the moment looks as if it may be Atticus.

Speaking of marriage to Atticus, when we were younger, just kids, we had joked about that. It would be us getting married in a church, me actually in a dress looking beautiful, and him in a tux. That always got us to laugh. We could never picture ourselves like that, he said I would be married in the tux and my husband wears the dress. I usually said a remark of that being him, that kept his mouth shut. He was the boy next door after the girl couldn't have or the whole best friends have feeling more for each other. It was all a joke, right? Yah right, it doesn't seem like it.

"Thank you Mallca," Vaughan said hugging me.

Hold the phone! My, little brother, the rude twerp, just hugged me? This was unusual to see us do, quiet a rare sight actually. Someone should take a picture, almost should.

"Anytime," I say telling him that I'll always be there for him when no one else is. When I said it, I mean it and it can be about anything. He finally released me seconds later. We glanced at each other to see smiles. It was only a glance because I thought I heard someone call my name. I asked Vaughan if it was him or our parents. It didn't sound like them, but the voice was familiar. To answer he shrugged his shoulders.

"Mallca!" I heard again. It sounds if it came from outside and only one person could be there. I went to my window to see Atticus looking outside looking up.

"What?" I asked opening my window to get my head out. "Come outside really quick!"

I nodded and made my way downstairs. I had the choice of using my window, but I learned my lesson when I was ten. Similar situation and I fell spraining my ankle. The doctor said I was lucky I didn't break it. My parents were also upset, but since I was injured the anger died. As I went to grab my jacket my parents asked where I was going. I had no reason to lie, so I said Atticus needed to talk to me. I got the okay as long as it didn't take too long. When I walked out it could have been pitch black except for the porch light and street lights on each house. Atticus jumped up the steps showing his face having the look of worry and fear searing a crossed it.

"What's up?" I asked. He was breathing heavy, probably from running over here, because he was having trouble getting his words out. Just words bunched together as one, jibber jabbers mainly. I couldn't understand a word he was saying. The last time I was confused by people's words was when they used words not in my vocabulary. Like anyone in my position, in the situation, I told him to hold off and breathe before speaking again.

Finally allowing his lungs to catch up with the rest of him catching his breath he said words I wished not to have heard,

"Bethany's thirteenth birthday was last week and when we arrived home my mother received the letter about her Predetermine."

"When is it?" I had a concern for Bethany. She was the little sister that I'll never have, however, I don't see Atticus as my brother much anymore.

"November twenty-forth is her date," he replied. I knew it would be before the end of the month, but that date. Hearing him say that date I leaned my head against the beam of the porch.

"What's wrong?" Atticus asked noticing my sudden distress. At first I didn't answer. "Mallca, what is it?"

"It is the same day as Vaughan's," I confessed as I release my held breath. It showed like white cold fog in the November night.

"Seems like us all over again," he replied. I wasn't in the mood for jokes.

He just had to remind me. For a while I was forgetting this all happened between us with my mind focused on my brother. Figured, it is either him or Vaughan to ruin my nice moments. Oh well, cannot be helped.

"Yeah, it does."

By that time it was going on ten o'clock at night and both of us had to go home. I figured Atticus snuck out to see me, as usual, so he had to return before his mother noticed or how long Bethany could keep her busy. She never failed us. In my case I had to go back inside. I knew if it was the other way around I'd come to him, with Vaughan as my cover.

I walked inside rubbing my arms to place heat back into them. Even being outside for ten minutes got me cold. I tried not to show my depressed look to my parents as I went for the staircase. My body language and steps tell so much to concerned parents. Being that type of parents they noticed and asked. Sometimes I wish they weren't such good parents and left me to my thoughts.

"It's nothing." I replied trying to retreat upstairs to the safety of my room, which isn't true. My mom invades my room all the time so nothing can be hidden. My nothing means something while something means nothing. I know it doesn't really make sense.

"Is something up with you and Atticus? Did you two fight about something?" my mother asked.

Would she stay out of my personal life? I'm sure that is why it is called personal. What happens between Atticus and I is not her business, unless it affects the entire family. An example would be like if we got married. My father is good about my personal life and knows when he needs to pry and if I want him too. Sometimes I think they switch roles of parents where he is mom and mom is dad.

"No," I said getting a slight attitude by her question perturbing me.

"Then what is Mallca?" my father asked saving me from blowing my top.

"He told me that . . ." I started before getting interrupted by no one other than my mother.

"That he loved you! Then you were speechless and said you would think about it! He now noticed because of the match up of your Predetermines!" She was quick with her outburst before I had a chance to finish.

"No!" I yelled that was probably heard by our neighbor. Not only was that when my short fuse went, but I did not mean to scare or get upset with my mother.

"I'm sorry Mallca . . ." she apologized.

I told her it was okay and I should be sorry for snapping at her. I understood why she said what she did. Like me, since my Predetermine and being compared to Atticus had us all jumpy on one subject. This subject just happened to be my love life. It was a very touchy subject I never liked to discuss and everyones seems to be a part of except me. I will open myself to a lover when I'm ready or when I find the right one.

"What Atticus had to tell me was that Bethany's Predetermine is on the same day as Vaughan's," I finally got to say.

Both of my parents were speechless and had no comments about the news. I believe they saw what Atticus saw and had no reason to bring up. Since no one wanted to talk about this any longer I turned to make my way back to my room. I happened to see Vaughan's shocked face to learn what I had kept from him.

Me coming in the door must had brought him down to see what Atticus wanted to talk to me was about. Before anyone could say anything he ran back upstairs.

Never once did I mention about Atticus's Predetermine matching mine to him. I thought it would be too weird for him to see Atticus as his brother-in-law. I know I wanted to talk to him, but I knew he wasn't going to listen to me. Knowing him he would wait until I got close before slamming the door in my face. I didn't take the chance and I was glad because that was what he did. I know now from when I received wooden splinter in my nose the last time I fell for it and it hurt both my pride and nose. At the moment I don't care. I just walked in without knocking or caring about personal space.

"Knock much," he said like snotty brat.

"Not really. You should know that doesn't work for me in this house," I replied smiling trying to tell a joke that was oddly true. No joke about it being the truth, if it's not the bathroom, I will walk right in if the door is closed and there is something inside I want. That attempt failed in gaining him back. He usually laughs, but no reaction. It was plain sad and he left me hanging like a dummy.

"Look. I'm sorry I didn't tell you, but I wanted to protect you," I explained.

"Protect me from what?"

"From this being weird, you could see Atticus as more than my best friend. How would you feel if I told you we were dating? I know I would feel weird if you dated Bethany." He gave a look like he understood and I gave a good example. It is great and weird all at the same time when knowing this person for so long as friends and it all changes when they date your sibling.

"To be honest Mallca, I have been seeing that anyway and we all say it is going to happen, only if the Predetermine does not get in the way. Plus you know I can hide anything from people just as good as you can."

I knew what he meant by this. Atticus wasn't my only partner in crime, Vaughan was too. When we were younger, even now, we kept things are parents. Secrets such as actual test scores, who broke mom's lamp, and the list goes on. With Bethany covering for Atticus, Vaughan did that for me. That was another secret. I smiled and was glad he understood my reasoning. Also there was no door in my face! Then I noticed something about hiding things from people.

"Do you hide stuff from me?" I asked with a suspicious look and eyes. Vaughan looked nervous and could crack open sweating like a jogger doing a marathon.

"No…" he answered not looking directly into my eyes and peering around the room to avoid me. I've learned how to tell when people are lying. It's hard to escape me. Such a bad liar and will always be. This is why most of my sneak outs ended in me getting caught, but we do what we can work with.

"You do!" I said smiling and beginning to rough housing with him. My brother and I were the type of siblings that didn't stay mad at one another very long. Plus I usually won his side and usually the play fighting.

Both households, the Siyas and Issigna, had hoped the days leading to the Predetermine of the youngest child would go by slowly. They hoped for the sake to preserve their child's young, free lives instead to be devoured and gone in a blink of the Committee's eyes. All thirteen years of carefree life just swallowed up like it never happened in less than an hour.

It was like déjà vu the day of November twenty-forth. The exact same car ride, the same way to the same damn awful place. Strangely we were wearing the same clothes in the familiar scene of looking across the lot to see Atticus and his family. In this situation their only seemed to be one difference, it was neither Atticus's nor my turn.

We all met at the door and when inside to see children of thirteen years of age. Oddly I saw them when I came for mine. As we waited for our parents to check everyone in I noticed what Bethany had on. It was a dress I had given her when I grew out of that she said she liked. I'm talking bad about myself, but she looked better in it than I ever did. A reason probably was I never wanted to look nice for anything. I like my pants and wore them quite well. Make-up wasn't the substance I enjoyed putting on my face unlike dirt, where I would just slap it straight on. The girl in Bethany was what my mother wanted in her daughter; she was sadly mistaken.

"You look nice in that dress," I complemented sitting beside on a wooden bench in the hall.

"Thank you. I wore for good luck," she replied.

Good luck? How is my dress good luck? It sure it doesn't have special powers, if so, I want it back. The only feelings that piece of cloth brought me was the ability to not be able to breathe and the chills. Indeed it was pretty and that's why my mother bought it on sale when she disapproved of my ripped and dirty jeans in summer. I thought my jeans were fine. The color pink is not my favorite color, actually, I have a strong distaste for the color. It was held on the wearer by thin spaghetti straps with a design of small flowers coving the entire dress. When I mean not being able to breathe I really mean it. It was tight around the abdomen leaving no room to expand my lungs or diaphragm. A dress never suited for me and more like the cute girl next to me, which now I had to ask why?

"Why is it good luck?"

"Well . . ." She hesitated. *Didn't think I'd ask, did you*, I though. "You had a good Predetermine on your day and so since you can't be in there with me I hoped the dress will do it for me. You know as in giving me the same luck as you. I love my brother, but you're the older sister I wanted."

I was speechless and shocked that this little girl thought of me during a time like this. Most people want their family, but not Bethany. Plus I didn't think my Predetermine was that good anyways. I may get an illness and die, not only having the chance of marrying her brother. Knowing her, she would like that. This is why we are like sisters.

"Thank you," I said showing that her words touched my heart, almost making me cry. I gave her a hug hoping for more luck for her.

"I thought of a way you will also be there. Since you and Atticus will be together one day you are like connect as one heart. So basically where ever he is, you are too," she whispered in my ear during our hug.

I pushed away and gave her a dirty, but funny look. More like a face that said 'really'. Was she my mother or have they been around each other too often? I knew Atticus couldn't keep his trap shut; he never could. Or the possible reason that Bethany beat it out of him her way, meaning annoying him with stuff until he cracked. Either way, one was still right. Bethany giggled and we gave each other a hug before her mother called her because she had just been summoned. I figured now I would have to wait for Vaughan . . . I was wrong when I heard his name seconds later, Vaughan Hamel Siyas.

Chapter

3

Hearing my brother's name stopped mine and probably his heart dead in its beating tracks. I got from the bench and walked to my family as we prepared to go inside. It was like the same setting over a year ago, but this time I wasn't sitting in the middle chair in front of our state's committee.

Before taking out seats I kissed Vaughan on top of the head and gave a nod reassuring him. I got the typical brother response of gross and wiping it out of his hair like it was poisonous. I hoped it could be for good luck like what I did for Bethany.

Before the Committee entered a little girl at the of age of twelve entered with her parents at her heels pushing her along. The girl was blonde and seemed to be shaking out of her child heels. Wait until the poor dear has to go through her own, she'll be worse. Better way to say describe it is looking like Vaughan; who is shivering with fear inside, but trying to keep his composure state outside and slowly losing it. I would have reminded him to breathe if the Committee had not enter and I then quickly went to the back of the room to the spectator seat before I got into trouble from either my parents or them. With the Committee, their deal is interrupting or distracting the one being determined would be the one of the worst stunts to pull. They seemed to eye Vaughan for a while before turning to speak with one another.

"You have been decided!" a voice rang. Vaughan jumped and I closed my eyes. When I opened them I saw four people in black and no Illingsworth.

"You shall not marry nor date!"

'What did he say? Repeat that please!'I thought. My little brother doesn't get to experience love, just stay hidden inside his heart. Well at least he won't ever have to worry about getting a broken heart, but still.

"In addition, you shall be a chef!"

That's not as bad as the first, but still bad. My brother is picky when it comes to food.

"At first succeed then crash and burn after a mistake!"

Damn. I was hoping for this not to happen. This was getting bad.

"Then you will live successful after picking yourself up and live normally."

"Son of Arrington and Kenari Siyas, Vaughan, you have been predetermincd!"

The only woman of the four said the final words of the Predetermine. I had always been keeping a close watch on them. I noticed she was smiling at him when she said it. She must have felt the men were harsh on him and gave him relief. She must have a son of her own that did not go well.

When my eyes finally ventured to Vaughan his face looked if he was cut off of air supply. Little relief appeared when the black haired woman spoke at the end. My older sister feeling just wanted to take him in my arms and hold him as tight and not let go. My mother beat me to it. I wish I could switch Predetermines with him. I'm not sure if it is the older sibling talking to protect the younger, but does that matter? Just like before, even though I can't do much about it, I meant I would be there for him. This worry about his Predetermine secrets were over, but quickly another rose after the first dissipated. It was for Bethany Ann Issigna.

Like Atticus and I, and now Vaughan once did sit in the same seat in the court looking room. Daphnia sat beside her and Atticus sat in the back like I did. A small red head girl sat and watched with apparently with her grandparents, who were her guardians. That poor girl lost her parents; I hope I never know what that felt like until it was time. She watched intently how Bethany's would unfold.

"You have been decided!"

Bethany wished to grab her mother's hand, but found the sides of the chair more suited for her nails. Her sharp talons, as Atticus called them, left impressions on the sides in seconds. I wonder how only times they replace these? Lucky that is not her mother or there would be blood. If she went any farther her nails might touch.

"Search for years to find the one you love."

"Have three children, one will be a half to the other two."

"Keep a stable job in education."

"However live long, but in the lower class."

"Daughter of Daphnia Issigna and Father of the deceased, Bethany, you are Predetermine!"

I was relieved to hear that night that Bethany would be alright and safe for a long time. If anything happened to her I know not only would her family be crushed, but I would too. I can relax with Bethany so I can focus on Vaughan and hopefully not get in trouble. I see not being able to experience love like being a lonely wandering soul waiting for the end. With me having that part of his Predetermine I would at least been able to live with it.

Most of what adults say to me or what I have overheard is the worst is over when your Predetermine had been decided. They are not telling the truth. I bet they say that not to worry children. The possibility could also be that they got off easy, which is rare that someone gets. It's like going through a nightmare, that you can't wake up and must followed as long as oxygen comes in and carbon dioxide comes out of the body.

The question "what do you want to be when you grow up" should not even be asked. It gives kids false hope in their future jobs. However, the job portion of the Predetermine doesn't start until after high school so the only thing about it is worrying about which classes to prepare when you go on to learning the actual career. That is why you get the Predetermine before you enter high school. And that was where Atticus and I were going to school. Classes were going to be uninteresting because we didn't like our jobs to begin with.

I woke the next Monday sleepy and it seemed to be melancholy. I just wanted to sleep as I kept dozing off each time I went to get up. Skipping seemed like a good idea, but I would get into so much trouble. Not just my parents, but also the school. In addition I would never get away with it; I'm terrible at playing hooky.

The high school thankfully did not have uniforms so I wore whatever I wanted, as long as it fit dress code. Each day we had different classes to attend too. Today I had Chemistry, History, Art, Physical Education, and Geography. I didn't mind Chemistry; it was the other ones that sucked. I could never get myself into it. *Oh joy*, I thought then as I realized I would spend the next odd number of years falling asleep in class. I guess I had no excuse to say I'm tired.

I decided my favorite jeans, long sleeve shirt, with my winter coat on top. I carry a jacket with me during the day in case I get cold. I waited for Vaughan by the front door, who usually took his time then we would walk to the bus stop. I had always made sure that we got there early so we would catch it. Atticus and Bethany usually arrived when the bus showed up. For some time we went earlier than normal to pick them up. He complained about the wait. I looked out the window to see them running.

"Hey," he said sitting down in the seat beside mine and having his back against the window. We were the first stop so we always got a seat.

"Hey there," I replied.

"So another day of being bored. The weird thing in my first aid class I enjoyed learning CPR," he explained.

"Oh, that's good to hear."

I was too worried about Vaughan to even think of a better reply. Not only that, I was upset the Atticus was taking and living the job I wanted as a child. I've been the person to help people and never give up about it until I couldn't do anymore. What can I do with that job trait and with being an archeologist? Rewrite history books? Discover a dinosaur? Yeah right.

"What's wrong?" he asked. Damn; he caught me in the act.

"Nothing," I smiled shaking my head quickly and shrugging my shoulders.

"Mallca . . ." he sounded if I lied to him, which did.

"It's just Vaughan and that you'll be a doctor."

Atticus leaned back against the back seat looking straight forward, at me. He saw that I knew and understood it wasn't him or his fault. That was how it all came to be. As I looked into his eyes I saw that shine. That most likely means he has a plan and they never turn out working right. I rolled my eyes and asked. Knowing that I would do so Atticus jumped to my seat and I moved over to make room. He had the largest grin on his face. A part of me wanted just to slap it off or wipe it. I could not do that without knowing what was going on in his head. Whatever it was, it was crazy.

"I have an idea that will allow both if us to do what we want," he started, "How about you teach me and I teach you?" Now I was confused. I showed by titling my head. "We both know each other and are own skill and the others. So we both get to learn our wanted jobs and maybe we could consult each other from time to time."

I was right; both he and the plan were crazy! Well it takes a crazy guy to think of a crazy idea. Or is he in a way smart? I have motto I made up for what this situation is: stupid people do dumb things; smart people do crazy things.

"Are you crazy or need professional help? What if we get caught? You know what they would do to us!" I reminded him. I really don't want to ever see the prisons, not even for a field trip.

"That is why we'll be careful."

"I don't know." I was extremely unsure.

He looked at me with eyes that pleaded into mine. He seemed that he wanted to actually go through with his outrageous plan. He only needed to commence with it. If this was a court case his eyes and problem plead guilty while they only seem to be innocent.

"Okay . . ." I sighed. The grin returned and I knew that must have been the worst mistake of my life, no joke.

During the entire conversation I never knew what was going on four seats ahead of me. It would have been nice to know sooner than later. That I was not the only one about to break the Predetermine rule.

Vaughan and Bethany, being younger had to sit near the front of the bus. It was the bus system: elementary school way front like behind the driver, junior high school middle section, while high school sat in the back. Just as Atticus and I had our outrageous talk, so did they.

"Do you wonder what they talk about back there since it is just the two of them?" Bethany asked looking behind the seat toward her older brother.

"Who knows," Vaughan answered. He was never into what I was doing. I was his sister and stayed out, just like my room. However, Bethany was curious about other people's business and Atticus's and mine was usually at the top of her list.

"I bet they're talking about themselves. You know about their relationship and such," Bethany said jumping to conclusions.

"I don't think so. Mallca is not really into that stuff," Vaughan stated and I don't ever expect to be into romance. I'll marry just to stay out of prison meaning I will do what I have to do. Sadly Bethany and Vaughan began to have the same thoughts they did about us.

"Do you think about it?" she asked him nervously. Vaughan seemed shocked at what she had just asked him.

"Sometimes, but that doesn't matter now. You know, since my Predetermine," he answered.

Bethany just stared at Vaughan as he was answering her question. She saw how upset he was at what now seemed impossible for him to feel. He could never have that crush on the cutie from his math class that he talks about every time she does something that seems amazing. Well I'm not sure crushing counts, because you can keep that to yourself. I think about I can figure ways around his Predetermine without getting him in trouble. Even if he does I'll be there to back him up. If a girl asked he would kindly explain himself and hopefully they'll understand. I don't follow the rules because I work around them.

Vaughan's mind seemed to be searching backward away from his previous thoughts. This was how his life would be in ruins. It has seemed Bethany had a sixth sense for when people were troubled. She slowly placed her hand on his. He felt her touch he looked up to see her smile. He forced one upon his face and blushed. Was Vaughan having feeling for Bethany? She must had seen his blush and grinned like her brother. It must run in the family. Was my best friend's little sister falling for my brother? That is sweet and gross all at the same time. By that time we had arrived at the schools. Of course school was school. I actually managed to stay awake during my classes . . . barely.

When school ended Atticus came over...with his book bag? What was the point? We never did homework together and we only had a couple of the same classes so cheating off me didn't help him as much anymore. He put it as comparing answers that are stored inside his head. Yeah, deep inside where he'll never find them.

"What are you doing?" I asked.

"You forgot?" he then asked.

What did you forget now? Does he mean the time he scared me so bad that I cried and was afraid of a bed sheet for a month?

Because I won't forget that and I know he won't let me. Or is he talking about our Predetermines? I badly needed a hint. I don't remember unless it is important enough. Plus I was tired this morning so it is all a blur in my mind. Sometimes I don't even know what I had for breakfast in the morning. Actually, I don't.

"I think so...give me a hint," I replied admitting my defeat of lack of memory and needed that hint. I have a sponge of a memory to most topics, just not life or at seven-thirty in the morning.

"Our arrangements of our jobs and classes," he hinted. It seemed more like gave it away and I asked for a hint.

"Oh," I laughed, "Today?"

"Yes."

"Why?"

"I'm interested to know the facts of what you know about my job," he explained.

"Fine, remember that we have to be careful and quiet," I reminded. He nodded knowing fully what I mean. I knew inside he was calling me a joy-killer. I wish he would only say it to my face, which will never happen. We got down to studying and during that time it was weird that Bethany came, not calling for Atticus, but Vaughan.

"What's up?" he asked her coming out onto the porch, before any other words could be spoken or wait for a response Bethany hugged Vaughan. "What are doing?"

"I'm sorry. I had to let you know before it ever becomes too late that I have feeling for you," she said quickly, "I know that we can't be together now since . . . you know."

Vaughan was speechless about what Bethany has revealed to him. This was all new to him and after the Predetermine he didn't think this would ever happen or worry. Deep inside him imagined a girl confessing her likings to him since he could no longer be hers. Never in this idea did he ever imagine the girl being Bethany. Instead of pushing this heartbroken girl away he pulled her into an embrace of a hug. After a minute they released and looked into each other's eyes.

"Oddly since this morning on the bus I feel the same," Vaughan finally replied. Bethany smiled and they broke their hug and into tears. Vaughan again embraced her to silence her crying.

"But . . . now . . . we can't . . . be together," she sniffled.

"I don't care," he said. She went to protest before being interrupted. "I don't care what happens as long as I can be like the rest of the people here. I want to be in love once in my life. Not hiding behind simple words of a higher power. If I only get to do this only once I'm glad it's with someone who feels the same for me too."

It all seemed quiet with no one worrying. Well to be honest we were all breaking our Predetermines. I was the only one focused on not getting caught; I guess my best wasn't good enough. I don't know how they do it, but the committee always finds a way uncover who has broken the law. I never knew one of my nightmares at night would actually be reality.

Lights brightly flashed and sirens blared throughout street. At first I wondered what happened until I saw them pull into our driveway. A strong, forceful knock was at the door. My heart dropped to my stomach with fear as my stomach went to my feet. I almost told my father not to open the door. As he opened or more like it was opened for him the police swarmed in. Everyone inside my house was handcuffed, including Atticus and Bethany.

"By order of the Committee, the Siyas and Issigna families are to be arrested for breaking the laws of the Predetermine!" the chief said strictly.

We were carried outside and shoved inside a white van. There were already people inside, only about three. Still, adding six more didn't help that it wasn't very big in the back and could not hold many more. Most of them looked at the children getting in with suspicious eyes. Probably wondering why the youngest being only thirteen was doing here. The fear dwelling inside me was almost as bad as the kind at my Predetermine, but this was much worse.

Everyone was shaking from fear and I did my best to hide mine from sight. I wasn't sure if the panic and fear did this to my mother, but she vomited in trash can that conveniently placed beside her by a police officer when he noticed her becoming sick. Even though it was in the can it didn't take away the smell. I tried not to gag because that wasn't going to help. I questioned that I wanted to become a doctor? I can stand blood and guts just not someone's lunch that came back up to say hello. My father gently rubbed her back to calm her.

"Are you okay?" I asked moving beside her. By that time the cuffs were removed and my arms were free. It didn't matter anyway because I could still feel them on my wrist as they were extremely tight and left marks.

"Yes," my father lied. I didn't have to look at him to know that he lied to me as my mother gave him the look to tell me the truth. "Your mother is pregnant."

That was how my mother and father broke their Predetermines. I never even began to think about that with all that had happened. They were only supposed to have two children: myself and Vaughan. I didn't know what to say as if my tongue was paralyzed. I would open my mouth, but nothing.

"How long has this been . . . ?" Vaughan asked for me.

"Four months," my father answered. The back became quiet of a while before the silence was broken by my mother. It was weird, for being four months along her pregnancy she still just looked like she gained a few pounds.

"What did you do?" my mother asked finally being able to talk with s fury hidden in her tone. She is talking to all of us.

"It was my fault Mrs. Siyas. I convinced Mallca to study my job and I studied hers. If anyone is to blame it is me," Atticus admitted.

"No, I agreed. It's just as my fault as yours," I confessed. I knew my parents were disappointed in me because I should have known better.

"No Mallca!" Atticus snapped before my mother could. If the prison did not kill me she definitely would.

"I confessed my likings to Vaughan ma'am," Bethany said being only guilty of the heart.

"The same for me mom," Vaughan added.

My mother's rage seemed to calm down knowing that our reasons weren't dumb: two for the job and two other's for love. Plus like she helped in the matter, she loved our father and they loved kids. She had no reason to be angry as we knew what we were getting ourselves into and no offense, she would be a hypocrite. If she was outside standing, not here sitting with us, she would have every right to be angry. As the van pulled away I heard a woman's screams. Atticus and I stood up looking out the two windows to see Daphnia chasing after the van. Inside the van was her whole world. The last image Atticus had of his mother was her running after us then being held back by a policeman.

Chapter

4

Atticus never allowed Bethany to witness what he had seen that day. As her older brother he wanted her last memory of their mother to be her telling her she loved her before coming to where she never should of came. The memory of her running after her children could be too much for the girl to handle as they are everything to each other since the loss of their father and husband. If only I had watched for the signs and stoppped it so that Bethany and Vaughan would be safe. Neither of the Issigna kids should have come to my house that day. The possibility of that could have prevented that mess. No, I needed quit blaming other people, it was my fault. Only if I didn't say yes and stuck with my ways. I had to let this all get to me and break me for that moment. Then all I knew was I must protect them.

After a seemingly endless ride we finally stopped. I had fallen asleep on my father like most daughters do. The sudden jerk woke me up off his shoulder. Actually I slept better right there then I had in a while or those weeks. My blurry eyes showed Vaughan with my mother. On the other side was Atticus with Bethany's head on his leg. They looked like the sibling souls that only had each other after death. Everyone looked so peaceful, I would have hated to disturb them all . . . I had spoken to soon.

The double doors of the van opened. I expected to be blind by a bright sun, but the lights were light poles shining down. As I got out the sky wasn't blue, but a dark night with no stars and barely a moon.

One at a time we exited the van to see our new transportation to the prison which was our new home for who knows how long. The prison was number 17-70. I do not know the reason for the numbers as my guess is a fancier was then saying one, two, and three. I also came up with the reason as this is section 17, prison number 70. These prisons are either located in the middle of a desert, a forest, and just about anywhere as long as manual labor could be forced. Just depends on the terrain you happen to live at the time. We went to the forest sector.

Several different pick-up trucks with empty backs had lined up at the gates waiting. We were set into an assembly line and prepared to be loaded. Before a prisoner was loaded for transport they were stamped. This wasn't your smiley face that said have a nice day that just washes off with water or rubbing alcohol. With this stamp alcohol would make it burn, like it didn't do that already. It was burned onto the skin like branding cattle that was placed on the upper left arm. The branding was more known as the cruel and painful way to receive a tattoo. I guess it can serve as a reminder to those who get out that this is what happens when the law is broken. Just only few ahead of me stood this guy scared out of his mind. He looked like he could jump from his skin any moment and dart. Again I spoke to soon again being right as he snapped.

The tall dark haired man jumped from the line pushing people out of his way running back the way we all came in. Unlucky me, I was included in this pushing. His hand pressed on my shoulder pushing me back. If he was like a more muscle type of guy he could have dislocated my shoulder. I braced myself to hit the cold ground. Instead I found my upper half in the arms of Atticus. He was thankfully behind me. He smiled and nodded as he began to lift me to my feet. As I was just about to have my footing, but gunfire rang out when I was still relying on Atticus's support. It caused everyone to jump and Atticus dropped me. I landed on my tailbone on a rock. That would bruise later I had thought to myself. I turned to look behind me to see the man who push me fall to the ground and die. I then turned to the opposite direction to see a man with a gun and the barrel smoking.

"See that! That is what happens if you try to escape. For you stupid people that means, you will die!" he yelled. Typhus Batson was the name of the person who said that to us and had no problem killing that man who tried to escape. He was the cruelest of the guards there. Of course because being head he has something to prove to everyone. I had already known I would be his enemy. "Now back in line!"

As we got back in line I ended being in the worst spot, the next one to go. From what I could see they gave different symbols for each person. The symbols were from animals to simple objects, just something to call you instead of your name. Calling by your name gave a person a place as your own individual. First they would look at your file and decide what you should be branded. The device was something I had never seen before. After deciding they put in the name that changed how the stamp looked. Batson looked over my file then into my eyes. Like Atticus he had a grin I just wanted to slap off. I held my hand.

Another guard then grabbed my arm holding it revealing the upper portion. I saw the stamp come my way and began to struggle. Through my two eyes I saw the stamp come closer to my dark complexion. I could feel the heat radiate off and barely start to press down. Pain, excruciating pain went to my bicep and then the rest of arm. Eventually the pain went to the rest of my body. As I went to scream another guard put his hand over my mouth. It muffled my scream to a down volume scream, but anyone near me could hear me. My screams transformed into silent whimpers. As painful as it was for me to endure it was probably was harder for my family and friends to watch.

My whimpers stopped after being lifted and tossed in one of the trucks rather hard. I couldn't stop my feet. and I slammed into a tall, muscular black man. He turned with anger and glared. Comparing his size to mine it seemed like he could snap me in half with one hand tied around his back and he only used his index finger. My face still had tears running down it and I was as a mess in every way. I stared up into the man's eyes to see him in pain as much as I was. A wave of calmness overcame his face when he looked upon my face.

I held my left with my right. I knew I couldn't cry anymore no matter how much pain I was in. I just had no more tears to give out and only wrenching screams would come. Out of my traumatized ears I could hear the screams of the other people who unfortunately came with me. People who I loved and cared about: Atticus, Vaughan, Bethany, Mom and then Dad. With my distant eyes I saw their crying eyes and hurt faces. I can feel empathy for all of them, even the people I don't know. I wish could get to them as I was separated unable to move.

The trucks felt like they had twenty people in each and was supposed to hold only ten. They are half of each other and that made a difference. Everyone had to stand because of this set-up. After an hour my legs felt as if they could give out from lack of strength and my weary eyes sagged. Mainly caused by the fact I used all I had to fight what I couldn't stop meaning the crying and pain. No one spoke the entire trip like I expected anyone to do so anyway. All was quite from any living humans. The only sounds came from around us such as owls hooting, tires against dirt roads, and the wind running through the trees. However every once in a while I did hear the crying of people.

To make this situation even worse the smell of rain filled the parts of my nostrils that were not already taken by the dust from the road. That was all we needed. Most of us were already cold and tired. Why not add water to see where that will grow? I really doubt our spirits would grow with a little water. As I feared it began to rain.

Cold water dropped from the cloudy night sky as if someone decided to take a shower. It poured as people say like cats and dogs. It wasn't the kind of water I remembered from a shower.

This actually hurt when it pelted my skin and in seconds everyone outside the truck was drenched head to toe.

I turned as much was allowed to see Atticus with his arms around Bethany protecting her. Lucky they were near each other. None of my family was remotely close to me. That came from me getting pushed into going first. I could see vague images of them, but no full view. Probably had something to do with the water in my eyes and the people. Of what I could see of my family they were at least together holding on to one another tightly. That made me happy and forget the present situation at the time. I knew they wished me to be there with them in the huddle. Strangely I didn't feel the same. I felt like I wanted and needed to die. I even went as far as thinking I should have never been born. At least they should have been given a different child so it did not break Predetermines. They would not be here if it wasn't for my choices. Agreeing to the demands of Atticus and not sitting with Vaughan that morning. Screw the rules, I should have been smarter.

On the way I could feel the ability to move return. This was actually a bad thing. The less people meant that no close connection to share body heat and more room to get away and to shiver. It seemed I was the only one who was. Yet I was still unable to reach my family. Faintly I could hear my teeth chatter. It looked like I was crying from the rain hitting my cheeks. To be honest a couple of those drops did not come from the sky, but my eyes. Knowing me if asked I would blame it on exhaustion and my eyes were watering. I didn't expect what had happen next in a lifetime.

A sudden burst of heat filled my body tightly that kind of felt like I was placed inside a rug in a taco style. Could have been the possibility of my muscles contracting and the burst of heat people feel before they die, but that wasn't the case here. I looked up to see the man I bumped into earlier. He wrapped his arms around me. They cover my entire upper half. I wondered why he did it. Did he feel sorry for me?

There I began to understand why it had become easier to move earlier. Only one word could describe it, death. People were either pushed or jumped to save them from what will soon come to them. I see the reason, but it makes you scared and willing to commit suicide. If you didn't want to come why did you break your Predetermine then? I saw it unjust. People would be eaten or just die painfully there. Again it seemed like a good way to escape, but would it work? Even so guards from another truck behind us would either run over you or shoot you in seconds. Or cruelly let nature have its way with you. If your truck was last you could have a slim chance to survive.

After about what felt like another hour the truck finally stopped outside a barbed wired prison with a steel gate. Inside were eleven long barracks. They were all color coded in a dark shade. There was also a decent white looking on that belonged to the guards.

"Alright get off!"

The truck which we were loaded in started with twenty people, but that number was reduced to fifteen. Five people died on the two hour trip from our transport and thirteen was the total combining the last two. Luckily I did not know any of them, but still sad that they had died. The guy holding me let go and got off with me. He treated me like a security guard at the store with a small child looking for her parents. He even held my hand. Before I went to find my companions I hugged the guy thanking him. He returned it knowing how grateful I was for all he had done for me.

It didn't take long to find my mom as I thought. Well it helped that she was practically screaming my name hoping I would I answer. If I didn't it would mean I was dead. As I appeared in her line of sight she ran and taking me into the embrace tightly.

"I was afraid you died," She said softly with her voice which she seemed to be losing.

'Love you too mom,' I thought sarcastically. I felt kind of insulted by her thought that I died. She really though I would allow weather to take me down, unless it was lightning then yes the weather got me, but still, no way in this lifetime. It would take more before I allowed my lungs to give out its final breath and my heart's last beat. That was not that today. I was too cold to answer her. I also wouldn't know what to say to her comment. Saying love you too would be mean.

The color of the building represented what section you belong to as a way to tell if we were in correct areas. Also it told which task we would be given to complete each day. This was no learning prison telling us what we had done wrong and you're free to leave with passing or good behavior. It was a labor prison. Everyone's work was in the range of collecting and preparing supplies to prepare for shipment. Everyone in our truck was placed in red block. We were the people to collect supplies and clothing materials. Those were only some of the jobs we were assigned.

We went only with the clothes on our backs. The only addition to our wardrobe was a bandana scarf. The color told which block we were in and it was never to be taken off. Mine was red and black that was in a checkered format that was a mixture in some of the squares. This means both fire and coal. Vaughan and Atticus also were also wearing the same scarf as we were all in the same work section. While the others were in the section of manufacturing supplies out of the resources we brought. They had red scarfs with white checkered pattern. You could call us the suppliers. The next day was the first day of work.

The housing was nothing more than beds lined up with a small pillow and a piece cloth to use for a blanket. I didn't care as long it was a place for me to sleep. Sleep was all my aching body wanted. Where I got it did not matter, as long as I got it. I would fall asleep in a corner if I could. As my eyes fell so did I on the cot. No one said a word as soon they all did the same.

A nightmare woke me that night from a decent sleep. I really didn't wake from a nightmare; I woke into one. I thought this all was nightmare and I would wake up in my bed at home. It was a long one that still continues when I decided to wake up. Cold sweat ran down my face; I was scared of what was to come. When will this nightmare be over? I looked around as my eyes adjusted to the dark to see everyone was asleep.

"I'll keep you all safe." I promised myself.

Before the darkness of sleep took over again I glanced at my arm for the first time since I received my mark. There imprinted was the image of a wyvern.

Chapter

5

Time had raced by so fast that I lost track after the first couple months. It was strange when my mother came up to me one morning telling me happy birthday.

At least I knew that someone was keeping track of the time that passed. Without a notice I was already fifteen. I had been worried about work and my priorities I forgot. Then I remember that the month was August and my mother had only one month left until my baby brother or sister would be born.

That month went by fast too and it was now September. Mother was nine months pregnant and she wasn't looking very good. She wasn't allowed to work which we all appreciated for her benefit. For being at her full term she seemed skinny. For a while I have been giving her some of my food each day when she wasn't looking at meal times. I don't think she noticed. To her the extra food could be from the prison supervisors or my father. As long as I could keep them both in good health is what I cared about.

It was about her due date and so I have been told this was when things really turned down. Like any other day in this damn place that represents hell, where we got up at six and ate breakfast until seven. Afterwards we worked until noon then having lunch or a break. You only got lunch if you deserved it by giving your entire work load for the beginning of the day. An hour was given there before we worked until six and the same rule to receive dinner. I usually got in my load; it was Vaughan I was worried.

He had slipped up a few times and almost didn't get a meal which for a kid like him that matters. I had to either give him some of my extra supplies or shared my meal. He saw it as charity or being the older sibling which was so unlike me apparently. My viewing of the subject was that I was looking out of him only so I can make his life hell when we get out of here and these idiots were stealing my job too. Vaughan also thought that mom and dad told me to do so, but the truth was no one told me a thing. Being stubborn as he is he did not believe me when I said they didn't tell me to do anything.

To never make sure that he never fell behind in work Vaughan tried to stay with Atticus and me as we did our runs. Atticus never had the problem of lacking supplies or keeping up with me. One day we didn't notice that he had fallen behind.

"Vaughan Siyas, the cat! You did not complete your supply income! No meal for you!" a voice roared. My heart jumped from the statement. Slowly he walked over to me not shocked by this fact. "Vaughan. You completed it. You were behind me the entire time," I said as he reached me. "I'm going to go talk to him."

As I got up someone grabbed my arm pulling me back down to my seat. It was Vaughan.

"No, he's right. During the time of gathering I fell behind because I got tired. Without you noticing you left and the next thing remember was you returning. So I made it seem like I was with you. I tried to get back ahead, but it was pointless. I'm sorry Mallca," he explained. He was about to cry like I was going to mad at him. Why would I be mad? He did nothing wrong.

Looking at him, hearing his explanation made me realize this was such a sick punishment. This boy wasn't even fourteen yet and he was doing a man's job. Without a second thought I slid my plate in front of him.

"Take it. I'll be fine," I said smiling.

"No," He denied shaking his head.

"Yes," I commanded in a soft tone. He saw I wasn't going to touch it so he nodded and began to eat slowly like he just got into trouble. As he ate I looked at Atticus. He smiled and so did I. I was proud of what I did, but one of the guards was not as pleased as I was.

"What do you think you are doing? I said no meal!" the guard said about to take away the plate.

"What does it look like? He's eating," I snapped moving my arm in the way, "the plate is mine. I don't want it and you don't want him weaker than his is already because of hunger. Do you? What is the point if someone still takes the fall?"

I know it sounded rude, but Vaughan and I knew it was the truth. Truth was actually I kind of did want the chow, but I couldn't let Vaughan see that. They weren't losing any food with this so I didn't see the problem. One of us still was taking the fall of an incomplete income of supplies.

The guard saw this as well as I and he was no one other than Batson, my worst enemy. He has been out to get me for some reason since that day I arrived. The look of disappointment was across his face. I had made a valid point that he could not argue. That made me smile. Could have been the best part of my day, or anyone's who was watching. Watching the head and toughest guard get put down by a fifteen year old. Silently he left with little pride I left him.

"Thank you," Vaughan said.

"Anytime and I mean it, okay?" I replied. He nodded letting me know the message had clearly gotten through to him. I was not going to let anything bad happen to him, ever. At least as long I was with him and still alive. Before we knew we had to return to work. Now we had to gather wood. This time I was going to make sure that Vaughan stayed with me. How could I be so stupid and not look back to see if he was still there?

Since then I looked back for Vaughan often more then I usually did. After the twentieth time in an hour it seemed to perturb

Vaughan. I decided that I could ease up some; that was a mistake. On our tenth run I heard the sound of a dropping of wood on the ground. I turned to see Vaughan's arms trembling and his gather at his feet. Quickly I kneeled down to help before anyone noticed, but I was too late to do anything.

"You think you can con food out of people and then slack on your work!" Batson barked. Vaughan looked too scared to even try to answer him. I gave a small nudge to focus him.

"No sir," he answered nervously and silently with his head down. If they were dogs the alpha male would have the young pup with his tail between his legs. And I was the older sister to the pup waiting to strike wanting to fight for dominance. I thought it was about time for a female to take charge.

"Well I'm sick of letting you get away with it! I think a punishment will change your ways!"

All three of heads shot up as he finished these words and ending with punishment. From what we have witnessed it could be from basically anything as long as it brought pain. Two weeks ago a man got punishment for fighting back in a fight between him and another prisoner. The punishment was that they each got a burn to the face. Then another guard walked up as Romone walked out with a leather whip. I couldn't just stand there and allow this to happen to my brother.

Right before Batson I slammed my pile of wood down at his feet. The young warrior dog became a wolf and was ready to strike. Both mine and Vaughan's wood were in the muddy ground and were ruined. The water in the mud was from the rain yesterday and would cause the wood to rot. Batson's rage that was toward Vaughan left and concentrated on me like earlier when we were having a stare down.

"I have had enough of you girl! Fine, since you're about protecting this maggot you'll take five too!" he yelled. He did not just call Vaughan a maggot. First of all he should of taken a look in a mirror and rearrange his face not to look like a bug. His oily greasy hair, his pale colored skin tone, and the scars on his face which was a face only a mother could not even love. Made him look like if he was a dead guy and there was actual worms wiggling around in his thick skull. Because of the thick skull he doesn't have much of a brain to fit inside his cranium that barely fits on his shoulders. Finally, something that made sense.

Still Vaughan was getting five whips too and that was not acceptable in my case.

"You're like your family, except you are much stronger. Your brother the weak bug, your father the mindless fool, and your mother the pregnant slut!" he insulted to my face, actually in my face making me rather uncomfortable.

Atticus also looked uncomfortable with Batson in my face. To him it looked as if Batson was in some sick way flirting with me. Atticus, who thinks he is my big and bad protector did not like that. However, for the sake of where the arguement was going he kept his possessive and protective nature down.

My temper then got a hold of me like he released the darker side of me and it finally got to take over. He insulted my family. If he had said anything about me, I could not have given a damn what it was. Going as far as my family was where he crossed the line. This time I didn't hold my fist as I punched him in the jaw. I thought I could help him with his face problem. When I struck I heard a crack or a pop sound. Down he went to the ground with me standing above him victoriously breathing heavy.

The whole prison was silent and no other guard tried or thought to approach me after what I did. All in shock at what I had just done to the head guard, the person they all were afraid of. Batson rose in pure fury all in my direction. When I got a look at my handy work I saw I dislocated his jaw. I didn't think I hit him that hard. What was gross was when he popped it back into place with just a push on to his crooked jaw. With his monstrous hands he slapped me to the ground. My face was numb and it stung. Atticus and Vaughan had jumped out of their skin when it happened. I was not going to let tears roll down my eyes especially on top of my beat red cheek.

"For that you take his licks too!" he demanded, "Grab her!"

Romone and another guard we learned to be Maurus grabbed me and dragged me to the center of the area. My feet left marks telling where I had been. A couple areas anyone could see where I struggled, but they were too strong for me. He didn't do it right there because he wanted everyone to watch in order to make an example out of me. Behind me I could hear screams.

"Mallca!" Vaughan projected at the top of his diaphragm. He repeated my name several times before he tried to sprint after me. He did not even get a foot loose before he was grabbed by Atticus. He was holding him back from making a huge mistake and meeting the same fate as me. I was held by my arms with my back facing Batson.

"This is what happens when someone decides they can mess with me," he stated. He gave this speech every time someone was punished. It was getting old and it was sad that I can almost retell it by memory. I was tempted to start saying or mouthing it with him and sort of did. However, I swore I heard a snicker from one of the guards. I wish he would just do it already. "The punishment is ten whips!"

Damn, but I knew what I was getting myself into the first night promising myself to protect my family, including the Issigna duo who I considered family, from harm. I composed myself bracing against what was to come. Without me even looking at the son of a bitch, that was probably true, I could see the smirk of pleasure across his face and the pullback ready to throw the whip.

With the crack of the whip came the unbearable pain of the slash. I could feel the whip slash my shirt and slap my skin. Not only that, when it was brought down it snapped my weak hair holder and my hair fell covering my back almost touching the ground when I fell to my knees. Within seconds the second came and my back, hair, and top were now the color of my scarf, stained or beat in red with my blood. I had to admitt that Batson had good aim to hit the same spot more than once. Also with the strength of the whip it cut some of my hair. With each whip afterwards I felt like they urged me to cry out. I was not going to let him hear me scream in pain, however, by the fifth one I broke.

Atticus's and Vaughan's eyes could not endure to watch anymore as they quit looking after the second. I would not blame them. They could not stand to watch the torture inflicted on me. Atticus saw that he could do nothing while Vaughan thought it was his fault. I don't know what made them glance a second time.

At whip number seven it seemed like I could not feel my back anymore as it was painless to the touch of the whip. Was my skin that tore up and numb to not register the pain or was I getting used to it? After whip nine I had enough of them holding me. Their grip wasn't as strong as before so this allowed me break it and turn facing Batson. The tenth and final whip came across the side of my face on the exact same side he slapped me on. I then felt the pain again as it was a new area and my back was already tore up. The whip had such a force to throw me to the ground on my side. When I hit I breathed in taking in some dirt in my mouth, but it was what came out from my mouth. In reaction to get the taste of dirt out I spit making the dirt on the ground blow out and some blood emitting from the side of my face and my mouth. I figured during the slash to the face I either bit my lip, tongue, or both. I could have just laid there and died, but I could not have done that.

The entire crowd jumped at the sight and the action. I had the guts to turn to my punishment and take it head on, more like face in this case. No one else could have done what I just did. I was known as the child to stand up for anyone even if I hardly knew you. I thought I had protected my family from pain, but I was wrong. During my time of pain and screaming it was also another's. I shared this time with a woman I knew as mom and her name was Kenari Siyas.

Chapter

6

A sharp glare from my eyes to his and his to mine. I saw in his that he did not look happy. The last action he expected was that I would turn and face him. Batson didn't show it, but he was shocked. Including myself, I was shocked too that I actually did it. I thought about, but I guess that's enough. I guess the saying "actions speak louder than words" was true.

A wet liquid streaked down my face. Blood dripped off my sides and chin onto my shirt. I also could feel it roll down my neck. Like my shirt was not ruined to begin with. It was going to leave a scar, but lucky I could not see the other nine every time I looked in a mirror.

By the loss of blood or exhaustion that made want to fall back and lose consciousness. Before Batson left he whipped again at my feet startling me. In addition to that I fell into the dirt face first. I was not lost yet to the world. The thought of dirt in my wounds did worry me though. The last sight I saw before passing out was a guy come up to Vaughan and Atticus telling them something. They responded by running away . . . forgetting about me. Then I felt myself being lifted and dragged with toes trailing behind me again.

The boys ran as fast as their weary legs could let them back to the barrack we were housed in. Everyone was outside and guards forbid anyone to enter. However, when they saw the duo they opened the doors to allow them entrance. A loud scream met them as they entered. Bethany ran up to meet them.

"What's wrong?" Vaughan asked.

"Your mother is having her baby now. Your dad told me to keep everyone back here. Where's Mallca?" Bethany answered looking around for me. That was a good question. Atticus looked at Vaughan with shame when they realized they had forgotten about me. Then they remembered what had just occurred to me outside moments ago.

"Was someone getting punished out there? I heard a couple screams when Kenari wasn't," Bethany asked before any of her other questions could be answered. I never knew how she knew, but Bethany knew about my promise to protect them.

"Mallca was . . ." Atticus started.

"Mallca was the one being . . ." Bethany exclaimed in a crying voice before being interrupted and having their sentences finished for both of the Issigna children. The doors opened to allow two guards passage carrying my soft moaning body. They got their answers in the worst way possible at a time like this.

"Mallca!" Bethany screamed as the guards dropped me on the cold rock floor. I didn't feel a thing I was so out of it when I hit the floor. "Mr. Siyas!"

"Dad!" Vaughan called. He actually got to look at the damage that was done and a feeling of guilt grew inside.

Arrington ran out behind a curtain, which was made from a collection of the cloth we used as blankets, that was located a few beds back. He saw the group of kids hovering over a body and Atticus kneeling down to comfort the mysterious person in his eyes. I don't think he thought about where I was.

"What's . . ." he started then stopped his thoughts upon seeing that the person they were so worried about was no one other than his daughter. "Mallca!"

He pushed his way passed Bethany and Vaughan kneeling next to Atticus. Bethany and Vaughan simply just got out of the way as they could only do nothing at the moment. My father seemed clueless about what to do with this new situation. He already had one that needed attending to. Placing his hand under my chin he inspected the damage. His heart dropped to his stomach seeing my back then to the floor at the sight of my face.

"Arrington!" my mother cried in more ways than one. He was lost on what to do. Go to help his wife or stay and care for his daughter.

"I got her. Go," Atticus said nudging him. My father nodded rushing back to my mother. She was sweaty and out of breath.

"What's wrong?" she managed to asked before going into another contraction.

"Nothing," he lied. He was trying not to worry her with another problem; she needed to focus. She gave him the look I give when you lie through your teeth and I can tell. That explains where I get it. "It's Mallca. It looks like she was whipped."

My mother was speechless and she was about to answer him before being cut-off once again. Instead of words he got grunts and screams. My father said he cringed in pain from her squeezing his hand so tight. He described it as she was crushing the bones or the life from it. Moments later screaming became crying, from three different parties: both my parents and my new baby sister. Seeing the new daughter in their life made them forget about the one they already had.

"It's a girl," he said passing her to my mother wrapped in a cloth. She seemed too weak to even hold her. The sounds of crying brought a curious younger, now older, brother over. "Come see your sister."

Slowly he walked to them and my father gestured it was okay for him approach them. Sitting in his mother arms was his new sister and he already had one. They already had a daughter. Looking upon their happy faces upset him.

"How can you be so happy?" he snapped. Our parents questioned his outburst. "You have another daughter too. Her name is Mallca or did you forget? Are you just going to let her die so you can replace her?!"

His sudden outburst reminded them that I was there and injured severely. Kenari nodded to Arrington and he left to tend to his daughter. He came to my side before he was called back by Vaughan's cry.

"Mom!"

Vaughan grabbed the baby girl before our mom dropped her with the fall of her arms. Suddenly her breathing became short and her strength weakened with ever second that passed. Atticus nodded to him to go back as it seemed he was needed desperately. As my father left, Atticus sat next to me taking my hand once again. When my father returned to my mother she was looking deathly pale.

"I'm sorry, but I can't do this," she said with her eyes just barely open to see her surroundings. Vaughan moved with the baby still in his arms to the edge of the bed.

"Don't say that. You're going to fine and so is Mallca," my dad reassured trying not to tear up.

"No, I can't. All this was too much for me to handle and I'm afraid that I will not make it." She shook her head. "I love you Arrington, you are my soul mate. Please let her know that I love her and who I am. Vaughan, you are my boy and happy to sing to you whenever. I love you so much. Mallca . . . I love you. You are my first child and hope the best. Please don't allow me to see any of you soon. Again . . . I love you all . . ."

Those were my mother's final words to us, everyone in my family heard except myself and the baby. We had no idea what was going on. I never heard until I was told what she said to me. Inside I knew something was wrong. The sad moment was broke off when the metal door of the barrack opened again. Maurus and two other guards walked in. My father got up and went to confront them.

"What do you want? We don't want any pitiful condolences. Haven't you people done enough?" he said angry at what this pace was doing to his family. Maurus didn't say a word, but gestured to one of the guards to grab me. I didn't have the strength to fight back being so weak and the feeling of an unknown broken heart. Atticus still had a hold of my hand.

"No! You can't have her!" Atticus commanded tightening his grip on my hand. It felt like I was going to be pulled apart. A moan escaped from the pain I was feeling. The second guard took Atticus off and pushed him back. More like put him on the floor on his butt. My father on the other hand was not going to allow them to take another Siyas. Maurus got in the way of my father, but the tussle only last a minute as he was worn out already. During that time the guard with me in hold had the allowed time to escape out the door. Of course my father felt crushed as if a piano had been dropped on his head. He did not know whether to think of me alive or going to be dead.

I was unaware of my surrounding as I was moved to part of the prison I had never been into or what was going on. My mind was a blur just as a cloudy dream.

Did my mother just have my baby sister? Or was it a brother? Did she just die?

Still my back was in pain and the gashes burned all the way down to my bones. Muscle was torn and already tried to heal as that was the only way wounds healed here, naturally. I felt a cold damp cloth touch my back and later my face. I winced at the pain each touch brought. Disgustingly I felt strands of my hair being pulled out from the wounds. The continued slashes made my long hair become imbedded. Whatever moment to my back caused agony.

Was I topless or was I covered? Well of course I had my bra on, but still I don't know who was helping me. If so I feel embarrassed to be revealing. I'm not the type to be free and to be showing off. Yes, concealed is who I am about my gender.

It felt like minutes, but in truth it was hours before I flooded back to reality and actually even tried to wake up. My eyes opened to a kind of darkness. Lifting my head where I sat on my chin I saw my face was in a pillow. I hate to be resting unless I needed it. When I rose I found it difficult to move my back. I indeed had a tank top on which I was thankful for. I felt up my back side and found that I was bandaged from my shoulder blades to my lower back. Not only that I felt something attached to my face with a tightness pressing down on my cheek. My hand wondered up there to find that I had a bandage there too. Someone cleaned my wounds and patched me up?

"How are you feeling?" I heard a voice from behind. I jumped to a sitting position and saw Maurus in a chair in front of the cot. That probably wasn't the smartest idea because I got a head rush and winced.

"You did this?" I asked getting my head back.

"Yes, well not your back. I asked a female to do that for me. I figured you wouldn't want a guy doing that," he explained.

"Thank you," I said being confused, because I was. Maurus was being nice to me. Batson had made every guard hate me for some reason; what did I ever do to him? It must be something about my vibe toward him or just by looking at me. Anyway, Batson made sure every guard would have pleasure in watching me suffer.

"Why?"

"Why what?" he questioned. I didn't make it clear what I wanted to know.

"Why did you help me?" I clarified my question, "I thought Batson turned all the guards against me. Also is it not a rule that guards can show no kindness to us prisoners?"

Maurus looked at me with the look of that no one could hide anything from me, which is true. He saw that I knew more then I should know for a person in my position.

"That is true, but I'm not like other guards. I hate the way they make us live, by the Predetermine. Seeing these people suffer is sick," he explained. I nodded in agreement of his statement. "I should be asking you why?"

"Now it is my turn to ask why what?" I repeated his question from earlier.

"Why did you turn around on the last whip?" he asked. I knew why I did as soon as I did it. It didn't take long for me to give Maurus his answer.

"I wanted that bastard to look me in the eyes and do it to my face rather than be a coward and do it to my back," I answered in a strong tone. My eyes showed a glimmer if strength. What was keeping me going strong? Maurus seemed to be lost for words as I had given an answer that was difficult to compete with. At least I thought so.

"I'm sorry," he apologized putting his head down as if he had anything to be ashamed of. I was confused. Like I said, what did he have to be sorry for? I know that he had no choice in assisting in my punishment or it could end in getting his own or worse.

"About? I understand that you had no choice to . . ." I said before being cut-off by Maurus as he raised his hand to stop me from going any further with my statement.

"I know you understand that. I felt helpless having to hold you. Nothing I could do and the fact you were punished for the sake of protecting your brother. I'm sorry this happened to you," he explained, "Oh, and also about your hair."

What does he mean by that? My hair was . . . not there anymore. It was, but wasn't. I felt like there was something missing when I woke up. Even when I felt the bandages, but it just didn't connect. The feeling of my hair touching my back was gone. I knew my hair was not pulled up because there was no tug. Baldness was not the option because there would be an awkward feeling and my head would chilly. I had it, finally I decided to see what Maurus meant by my hair. The front of my hair felt fine, it was just when I reached back. The end of my hair was just passed the end of my shoulder blades.

"What happened?" I asked.

"Well . . ." he started, "your hair was in your wounds. We got it out, but the damage was done. The blood dries quickly and it matted. It was impossible for it to become clean so it had to be cut."

My temper was not going to come out. I wasn't mad at all. I knew why he had to do it or that would not be a pretty sight. On the table next to me I saw a hand mirror. Grabbing the metal handle I picked it up off the table. The back design faced me for a while before I decided to turn it over. I was scared to look. It could be bad. When I turned it I saw the bandage on my face. Moving around I saw what had become of my hair, my looks. What I saw kind of shocked me.

My hair felt it was at my shoulder blades; that did not mean it was. Did they use scissors or a weed whacker? The brown hair was uneven. The only untouched area was the front, still bangs on the sides. Looking from the front my hair started short, but went long. Gave my hair the appearance of it had been layered.

I did not look that bad actually; I could live with this haircut. When I placed the mirror back down I saw Maurus holding out a black elastic ring, a ponytail holder. I took it from his hand and scooped my hair up wrapping it. Some hairs were still hanging out. I checked with mirror again to make sure it looked good. My hair was fine.

"I'm also sorry about your mother," he apologized in sorrow. He was being guilty for me.

My heart dropped to the floor and weighted a ton. I know what he means. Those were no dreams. The questions I had asked were all answered to be yes. My mother was dead and my baby sibling was born. I expected what came next. Tears so suddenly filled my eyes and I coughed trying to get my breath from the shock. I found myself painfully running to our barracks from the white.

I rushed through the door, passed all the people to where my family was stationed. There I saw my father holding my baby sibling in his arms. I walked up and sat beside him. He looked at me in fear? Anger? What was wrong? He was confused. I could tell by his face. When he looked upon me he moved getting away from me.

"Get away from us! You won't touch this girl either!" he snapped. I know the new sibling was a girl and I was bewildered. Did he not recognize me?

"Dad, it's me," I replied, "Mallca."

"I don't believe you! Mallca doesn't look like you!" he told. He had a point that no one could have denied.

"Dad please listens to me! My wounds have been taken care of and my hair had to be cut because of the blood damage," I pleaded to him. His dirty face seemed to soften up, but even I could see he was not convinced.

"Prove it," he breathed out, "tell me something that only Mallca knows."

I had to think about it. I really did not know. Most people knew about my simple life. I couldn't say anything about family or friends unless it was something I did not want them to know. Maybe I could show him something.

"Do you know what my mark is?" I asked. He gave me a dirty look. "Do you know Mallca's mark?"

He nodded and I turned to my father showing my shoulder. I showed hi the wyvern that had been burned in. He jumped and his face eased into a smile. Holding the baby girl close he got up and hugged with care of both myself and the baby. I could see in his eyes he was happy to see I was alright and did not meet the same horrible fate as my mother.

"Where are the others?" I asked. Actually my father was the only adult in the barrack.

"Do you know how long you have gone?" he answered with a question. In truth I believed only hours, but I was not for sure. That was what I told him and he replied, "It has been at least a day and I would say it is around three."

My question had been answered. Atticus, Bethany, and Vaughan were working with the thoughts of me while my father was allowed to stay with the day old baby since her mother died. Gently we both sat back down on the cot and I stared at her. Ever since I saw her in his arms I wondered about her. Who she was? Right now the only name I had to call her by was my baby sister.

"What's her name?" I asked stroking my index finger across her little forehead.

"She doesn't have one yet," he replied, "I was hoping to get your opinion on that."

Why would he want my opinion on what her name should be? The girl is not my daughter and plus, I cannot have children anyway so what would be the point? The girl has a father to do that for. Well, if he wanted my opinion he would surely get it. What ran through my head weren't the sweet names everyone grows to love. I had come up with killer of mother or the name Lillith for short if it was too hard as the first was obvious. I almost said the name if I didn't look down at the child's face before speaking. She was not a killer who took my...our mother away from us; that was the prison's doing. This little one was an innocent soul born into this place where she had to live until someone among the four of us surviving gets out. The poor defenseless girl that now lives like a rule breaker and has nothing wrong to deserve it. I searched through the many names I knew mean close to this before I came the right one. For a while I never smiled, now the edges of my lips slightly curled upwards. The name wasn't Lillith and I believed my father would like the name too.

"What about the name Alaina?" I suggested my choice, "Alaina Kenari Siyas."

I gave her the middle name of the person who will be with her always, our mother. Her name meant innocence in my book because that is what she is even if others don't. Our father thought about for only a couple seconds before smiling. Apparently it was a good name, but in this family you'll never know.

"I like it," he replied. She finally she had a name and just in time to as the others came in. They ran immediately to father and Alaina. It was nice to call her by a name that suited her.

"How is she?" Vaughan asked before he noticed a mysterious, but familiar person sitting next to them. "Who are you?"

Just like his father, he or any of them did not recognize me. Had my appearance changed that much that I was a new person? Well I would have to agree because looking in the hand mirror

I almost didn't recognize myself with the hair and new facial decoration.

"Mallca . . ." Atticus implied coming closer to my face and looking into my eyes. I could feel his breath on my skin. It was warm and needed to be cleaned, but who doesn't need it. I nodded to his guess and he then pulled away, probably sensing how uncomfortable it was and smiled. Instead of words to express his feeling toward my present state Atticus hugged me. I swore I could hear faintly audible sobs. The cries stopped and Atticus let me go with his eyes had a red tint to them. Not even a minute went by before I was hugged by Vaughan and Bethany. Did everyone think the worst of me? Because I get relieved just being able to see them and probably the same for them. At least I was back and it was going to stay that way. That night I climbed into my cot unknown to what would happen next.

Chapter

7

No one could believe over a year had gone since that dreadful day of both being whipped and losing my mother. The only bright event that happened was that Siyas family received Alaina. On that day I wasn't myself, no one was except for Alaina. Maurus had been kind to bring food for her so we could keep her alive and well. It would do until she grew older. She still didn't have the slightest idea what was going on, who could blame the one year old. My father soon enough was required to return to his work so a kind older woman took care of her since she was unable to work. Either my father or I would come in on our breaks and check up on her.

Both Atticus and I were sixteen meaning Vaughan and Bethany were fifteen. I feel bad because I had forgotten how old my father was, I think he is about forty-three. It was close enough to it that I am sure. Again birthdays here were like any other day. No one ever got anything special and all you ever got if anyone remembered was some wishes for your birthday.

I had tried my best to keep myself out of trouble, but everyone knows that is not going to happen and it is very hard for me to do. Since then everyone seemed to have changed, that day had an effect on the people who it mattered to. Vaughan picked up and never got behind, Atticus was like me in being the guardian, and Bethany always made sure everyone was alright. It was kind of getting weird. I, on the other hand, did not change much, but I came more adamant about protecting them.

Since then I have only got slapped around only a couple times or four. It wasn't like I was keeping count. The gashes on my back have become scars that no one could look at without flinching as they try to understand the pain that I went through. Unlike the one on my face that no one could avoid except for me. Whenever I looked at my own reflection I saw the scar. Good news was it was fading becoming just a white line on my face. It wasn't me I should have been worried about.

It was late December and this was usually one of the worse times to work. It was in the winter where illnesses and cold weather were to be suspected and nothing was done about it. Work had gotten harder to accomplish and we were lucky most of the guarding staff understood this factor. During this time some of the manufacturers were moved to make clothing and under cloth for the people and guards. Out of the group Bethany was the only one that was chosen.

With her only being fifteen and as small she was it was difficult for her to do the muscle work, but the persistent people placed her as the person to slice the cloth. Basically a long knife that makes a clean cut on, well anything. A handle was there, but it was diminutive compared to the size of the knife. All the handle did was making the knife easier to move. Being small and not really muscular she became tired easy.

"Would you hurry girl!" a guard commanded. The strength of his voice made it seem he yelled the words right in your ear.

"I'm sorry," Bethany apologized, "I just get tired ..."

"No one wants your excuses! Just pick up the pace!" he yelled.

Bethany nodded and did what the guard asked. Even though she was tired she always tired her best and complied with what was asked of her. She was such a hard worker. However, in this dangerous job it is important not to rush because that it how accidents happen. The mind sometimes gets occupied with one task it forgets about the other it was trying to complete at the same time. It's basically the people who cannot multi-task very well. People do things without thinking as the brain is locked on another task and they do not always think it through all the way through. Being as intelligent Bethany was fatigue seemed to be her kryptonite.

"Bethany! Bring the cloth you just cut!" called a woman worker in her late twenties.

"Here is the next bundle for cutting coming down!" informed a man carrying the bundle and beginning to feeding it through opposite side of the cutter. The only thoughts in Bethany's dirty blonde haired head were to do what she was told and not hold the others back. With one hand she reached across to grab the already cut cloth. If the cloth is not cut as it is fed through it will back-up which will lead to what I have already experienced. Without thinking where her arm was she slammed down the knife.

Blood seeped into the cloth on both sides of the knife turning it either red or black red as blood. Pain did not register to her right away. She only wondered where the new color came from and was this blood? She looked down to only see the sharp blade sitting next to her arm. By instinct she lifted the blade to see blood. Looking at her arm the pain registered and she screamed like it would completely shatter glass.

Outside workers that were the rest of the group heard the faint scream, but we heard it. It was either a bundle of cloth or logs, I can't remember what I was carrying at the time, was dropped to the frozen ground in shock. No one said a word about having to pick them up and I did not even think about what happened the last time I did that. All we wondered is where and who was the girl's scream. Sadly I have heard that scream before when we were all at home. The scream reminded me when Atticus's sister fell out of a tree to the ground, almost 10 feet from the earth. I knew that scream was from Bethany.

Everyone quickly ran toward the warehouse to see what had happened. All I wanted to know if she was the scream I heard or not. I was sure she was and it scared me. If it was, I questioned if she alright?

The next sight I saw was a door flying open and Maurus running out with a bleeding girl in his arms that looked like Bethany. The worst part was Atticus was standing next to me the entire time this all went down. It seemed almost quiet when a familiar voice screamed in my right ear.

"Bethany!" Atticus was now the screamer. He then grabbed my cold hand thinking I was too frozen with the cold and shock to move as we ran after his sister.

Maurus had taken her where he taken me in my time of medical need. Since it was the white barrack we rule breakers were not allowed inside so we had to sneak inside. Luckily at this time all the guards are out so being caught was a minor issue. We did not have to search for where they had gone as the crying lead us straight to them.

Quickly he examined the weeping girl who was still frantically crying out in pain. I bet this was worse or just about the same as me. The blade had cut her at the wrist and she had visible veins which were sliced open. The constant bleeding was not only the only issue not just because the blade was operational, but rusty and never cleaned.

As we ran in Maurus stopped us from going any farther to the person who needed family and friends the most. Atticus almost rammed him trying to get to her; he would do anything for his little sister. Being a muscular guy Maurus had no problem holding his ground, it would take a while before Atticus actually made dent in the state he was in. Quickly before he hurt himself I grabbed his arm holding him back. The days of wrestling with him as kids and the labor paid off so I could hold him. He screamed at me to release him and I ignored him. He needed to be protected and not see his sister in this type of manner. I was also focused on the worried face upon Maurus. It actually resembled the sorry face he gave me when my mother died.

"Stop it Atticus!" I yelled in his right ear. I knew he heard me, but chose to blow me off. Eventually he calmed down and didn't try to be contentious again. This time allowed Maurus to say what was on his mind about Bethany.

"Your sister's injury hit an artery on the wrist and cut the vein. I can't stop the bleeding and it has already become infected. It is going too fast for me to catch it. I'm sorry, there is nothing more I can do for her now maybe except make her comfortable," he explained in a depressing tone.

My heart dropped, but Atticus's dropped even further. I could feel all his pain from losing my mother. I felt all the emotions radiate from him. As I placed my hand upon his shoulder he pulled away wanting nothing to do with me and rushed to Bethany's side. Maurus had done two things without saying anything to me. He bandaged her arm and covered it with a towel to spare anyone to look at the damage of the injury and told me he was sorry to see me go through another loss again. Blood soaked through both pieces of cloth and it had only been minutes.

"Hey . . ." Atticus whispered softly kneeling to her side and grabbing the good hand. Weakly she turned and smiled staring into his eyes.

"Hi . . ." she answered weakly. It was so soft that her simple greeting was almost inaudible to listening ears.

"You're going to be okay," he reassured her. Slightly she shook her head in disagreement with him. She winced, her pale face and skin tone, her head hurt as it became hurtful to simply answer her older brother.

"Don't lie to me . . . you are never good at it," she muttered.

"I'm not lying, Beth. All you need is a lot of rest and soon you'll be as good as new to get out of this dump," he said.

Tears not only had come to Atticus's eyes, but mine too. As much as we tried to fight them back we just couldn't. This must have told Bethany that he was lying to her. She understood why he lied to her. He was trying to be a good older brother and not scare her. All she could think to do was smile and remind him it was okay. For a while Atticus sat there and just talked to her as her time slowly withered away not knowing when it would reach the end. After the first thirty minutes I stood at the doorway only watching, wishing I could have done this too before I moved to a chair. Thoughts of the day of her Predetermine came to mind as I sat there and watched. All what she had to say about me came back. This girl somehow looked up to me and I felt as if I failed her.

"Tell Vaughan I'm sorry I could not be the one for him and Mallca, please don't get yourself killed," she said to me before moving to a more sensitive matter. "I'll miss you, all of you. Atticus, you were the best big bro anyone could ask for. I love you Atticus."

When his name left her mouth her breathing turned shallow and rapid. By then her beautiful skin tone had turned a pale having lost all color. As her breaths began to slow Atticus placed his hand on the side of her face. She was ice cold and she welcomed his warm touch in order to give her comfort. He leaded in kissing her upon the forehead. Bethany smiled as her eyes fluttered.

"I love you too Bethany," he replied softly.

Atticus hated them and was never good with good-byes. I remember when Bethany left for a girl's camp for a week. She begged me to go and almost talked me into it, but it would not appeal to me. It was a girl's camp and last time I checked with myself that is something I'm not into or at least I resent being. I also had the reason of someone had to keep her brother occupied since he would be lost without her. He came to my house everyday like I was her replacement and the girl wasn't coming home. They were overjoyed to see each other again. I told her what had happened and jokingly begged her to take her brother back. I know it is sad to put a funny memory on one like this, but I couldn't think about anything else. Actually I prefer to remember the good times then to think of the moments where I could burst in tears. Finally, Bethany Issigna stayed strong as long as she could and her blue eyes closed leaving her last breath on Atticus's hand.

"That's right sis, you just rest . . ." he begun. Atticus wanted to finish what he had to say, but not before the tears became too strong and they erupted. Neither of us were the criers, but we make exceptions for the ones we love. I knew what it may have felt like if I was there when my mother died. Actually I felt worse because I wasn't there. The loss would feel stronger than it does, but it seemed so similar.

Maurus could only allow an hour more with her and nothing more because we would get in trouble. Atticus wanted more time as to him she was sleeping. All he did for the hour was cry and speak what I could not understand. When the time came it looked like Atticus had to drag himself away from her with little help from my hand. Maurus then took her body to send it so it could be properly buried next to her father. It was nice of him to do that for us so at least we knew she would not be like the others and we could still visit knowing she was safe. Inside Atticus screamed to bring her back, but it was too late.

As we walked out a couple people gathered to pay respects to the youngest person to die in the prison so far. I was not sure where it started, but I heard humming. The others had joined in to hum to the sweet girl who only wanted love. It was soft tone of a tune I had never heard. I guess people who have been here a while have created their own tunes or communications ways. They showed so much kindness and this was going to make it harder to tell my father and Vaughan what happened.

"Where were you guys? Also I heard someone died today," my father said, "it is sad to think that people actually die here."

All we did was nod in agreement.

"Where's Bethany?" Vaughan asked. Instead getting an answer right away Atticus silently sobbed. "What's wrong?"

"I got it," I told Atticus rubbing his shoulder. I had to save him the pain of saying it himself as it was painful already. "Bethany is the one who died."

"What?" Vaughan voice cracked. Again all I could do was nod having to say some of the hardest words.

Vaughan also began to cry which started a chain reaction causing the calmed Atticus to begin again. My father didn't cry, but he cried in the inside. I started shortly after that only allowing the tears to drop. After they calmed I explained what had happened to her. Atticus cried for a while after and being his best friend told me to comfort him. I didn't as much as I wanted. It was also my turn with Alaina and I could really upset him if I do. He just lost his little sister and I bring over mine. I could see the reason was he wanted to be alone and it would be a while before he wanted anybody. However, during that night I heard Atticus my father while Alaina was asleep he asked could he hold her. I woke up the next morning with her in his arms.

It had only been two months after Bethany's death and I was beginning to get the old Atticus back. I could still see he was in pain, but that is a wound that will take more time or would never heal all the way. Just like the scars on my back and face that remind me I wasn't there when my mother died.

For the last week the people in my barrack have been acting suspicious by always sneaking out and around like they were on missions. Or they would have conversations that excluded the people who did not matter to the reason. Usually everyone knew what was up. It didn't take long before they included the trouble maker of the red barrack.

I learned that some of the people were going to try a prison break and escape. The people involved figured they had better chances out in the wild than in this place. Partly, they were correct. They wondered if I would be interested joining since apparently I do these kind of actions and piss people off. I thought it was good to know. Still that's was all I needed and Batson would have a field day with me. It would be like delivering my life on a silver platter to him personally. No telling what he would do if I tried to escape since I know what he would do if I stood up for myself and others. I declined the escape route for myself, but not for someone else. He had to get out before something happened to him, like Bethany, and I mean Vaughan. Every bone in my body told me to get Alaina out, but for her safety it was best to only push it with one. I informed my father who was first reluctant, but agreed knowing that his son would soon be free. Tonight was the night they would attempt the escape, hopefully nothing would go wrong.

It was late when they had everyone going to gather in the back of the barrack to begin to head out the back door. I walked with Vaughan having done what he asked. For the past week one or two people would take the chance to go out each night and create an opening in the fence made with supplies stolen from their work areas. All they had to do was open it and get out running for the protection of the thick woods. Home freedom would be waiting if they returned. A man that understood why Vaughan took my place was going to make sure that he escaped.

"I want you to run as fast as you can and do not turn around to look back. No matter what happens, you must survive," I said holding onto his shoulders.

"But . . ." he began to think of a reason to disobey me. Noticing that he wasn't getting out he nodded.

"We will all see each other soon. So don't worry that head of yours and think about yourself for once," I said knowing what he was about to say before he even had the chance to think it.

Again he nodded knowing that it was alright that he could leave. We could at least protect ourselves and stand a chance. Vaughan didn't belong here like I did. He just was just blinded by his heart and that's acceptable in my eyes. Sadly my eyes do not count in the judgment and if it did, neither Bethany nor Vaughan would be here. Actually no one would be here and if someone had to go I would make it myself. Then I was tapped on the shoulder and I turned to see a man nod at me telling me it was time. I watched at the side of the barrack as one at a time they made way to the opening. Vaughan was in the middle, being a child he should have gone first, but all these egoistic people.

It was a quiet night, as quiet to hear a pen drop, maybe not a pen, but a decently sized object or even footsteps. I heard footsteps in the distant coming this way. It was dark, but that doesn't mean you're invisible. My heart began to race and my breathing followed. I had to try and calm myself. Sending positive thoughts through my mind did not help as negatives just pushed them away. I could do nothing to warn them on the incoming company, which was most likely one of the guards on patrol, and they would be surely caught. I couldn't risk the operations success rate and Vaughan's chance. I knew I should have done something to stop them.

"Hey! What the heck is this?!" the guard shouted seeing one the other people try an ignorant move and make a break instead of waiting it out. If they did not get the guy I would.

Upon hearing the guard's shout alarms blared through the area waking everyone from their sleep. Our father feared for us knowing that his children were out there. Alaina who was wrapped in his arms hear the alarm and began to cry as the sound hurt her ears. It hurt everyone's ears that were near.

People had the instinct to run around like chickens with their heads cut off instead of remaining calm and trying to return to their or a barrack. The idea of returning to the barrack became obsolete as guards were everywhere even at the barrack doors to keep people in and out. This way they could see who was trying escape. I tightly leaned against the wall almost becoming one in attempt to hide myself. There I hoped for the best outcome of that Vaughan would get out or be okay.

All I can hear is the sounds of footsteps against the ground, shouting of the people, fellow inmates or guards, and then some screaming. I was in the dark about the commotion going on. I didn't even fear for my own safety if I was caught; it was Vaughan I feared for. As the silence came so did gunfire. I instantly jumped and gasped at the cracking sound. Without any control I jumped off the wall and ran toward the section which the fence was cut. When I arrived I didn't like what I saw; a few bodies on each side, inmates and guards, and the body of a brown haired child. My eyes widen as I realize that Vaughan was the only child that went.

"Vaughan!" I shrieked that ears would bleed if close enough. Sprinting from my held position I went to him sliding to meet him on the ground. I didn't care I ripped my pants and got dirty as it was nothing new. I even ignored the pain of bruising my knees against the stones. Vaughan lay on his stomach so I have some hope he ducked for cover. As I touched him he didn't move and when I turned him over to see a frightening sight that I have seen before. The sight of blood on his body as there was a bullet wound in his abdomen. Uncontrollably tears streak down my face from my blurry eyes.

"Mall . . . ca," he silently said. He has his eyes closed from the pain, but he knows it's me.

"Yeah it's me. You always knew," I replied brushing his hair gently with my fingertips. We both have always become calm with this.

"It is . . . so cold." When he said this my heart went dead and I felt him shiver. It wasn't from being cold, but from shock. I pulled his head onto my thigh to make it more comfort, hell, nothing could have helped him.

"It's going to be okay," I lied.

"Don't lie to me, Mallca?" he asked.

"I'm not . . ."

"Mallca?"

"Yeah?"

"Do you think this is how Bethany and Atticus felt not long ago?" he asked. He didn't just ask me that because it led to more silent crying or just the drops of clear salty liquid secreted from glands in my eyes.

Why wasn't anyone coming to help me? Where was Maurus? My little and only brother was lying on the ground dying and no one gave a damn about what happened to him! For a time of two months I thought the people here were better than that. At least they left me alone with him.

"I'll get some help," I moved on not answering that question because the answer was yes, this was exactly how it felt with Atticus and Bethany. I began to get up only making the smallest movement of placing my hand down when I felt someone grab my wrist. It was from the side that Vaughan was at.

"Please don't go . . ." I nodded and returned to my original position. I felt that I had to stop crying and get a grip on myself. I had to be strong for him.

"Mallca?" Vaughan asked again. I thought to myself, please do not be a question that I have to and want to avoid answering.

"Yeah?" I asked again.

"Will you do one last thing for me?" he asked.

"Like I said I would do anything," I whispered.

"Tell me what it is like to be in love? I want to know. What Bethany and I had didn't seem right," he asked.

I was speechless to his request. I don't even know how to explain it and I am not even in it. At least I didn't think I was.

"I'm not sure, maybe it was out of the being desperate because of never having it," I replied.

"Be quiet . . . I know how you and Atticus look at each other. What do you feel around him?" He placed in simpler terms and it actually made it easier to relate too.

Gosh Mallca think . . . what does your heart tell you about this?

"Well . . . you can never be away from them and if you are, you seem to be thinking about them all the time before you actually see them again," I started. I could see him fully indulged into what I was talking of or sadly it could be his eyes losing focus and looking to nowhere. "Every time they are near you, no smile is safe as it appears to show. When your eyes are closed they may appear in your dreams."

Vaughan did as I said and closed his eyes. I wonder if he saw anything as he had them closed.

He looked to see darkness that dispersed as a light came. A figure stood as if it was connected to the light.

"You act all goofy and try to find the blushes that are flushed through in the brightest red. Even love can be expressed through picking on one another and calling names."

Vaughan slightly smiled at my comment as that I meant for him and me.

The light came closer to his face and he could see the figure clearly. It was the only person that would want to see him again.

"I have always believed that love means being together. Together you share joys, sorrows and through that you come to an understanding. Sometimes you'll need to be there and other times you'll need some space, but you'll be there for one another regardless. No matter how many years later, you'll feel the same about one another. Love is the intense feeling that is said to be the strongest in the world."

The figure was indeed our mother soon joined by Bethany.

"I love you too Mallca," he said understanding that I mean I love him. I know that he want me to tell the others to know that he loved them too. As I leaded in to kiss him on his cold forehead my mother appeared to him. The grip on my hand released and fell. This was our last loving sibling moment and he ruined it with dying. I cried again as I felt like a just killed my younger brother. It was my entire fault if I didn't push him into going. I should have listened to our father. This will be the one I will not forget or even let myself. I understand why Vaughan asked me for my definition of love, he wanted me to make sure I moved on with my love life, my life, and to make sure he knew what it was as well as me. That the feeling he just felt was not some other emotion clouding his judgment, he knew it was love he felt for his family. Still, he got the one thing he could not ask me for, because he knew I couldn't for two reasons. I was not in the right state and someone else filled the spot. Vaughan Siyas got a lullaby to sleep to or in this case die.

Chapter 8

I fully understand Atticus the night Bethany died those months ago with all the pain and sorrow. It was my turn to be the distant one, and mourn for Vaughan. That night shortly after Vaughan died Maurus came in time to grab me pulling away to save me from getting into trouble. Like Atticus, who had screamed out calling for Bethany to return, I was the one to do it inside. I could not shriek out, if I did it would mean the end, and I could be meeting Vaughan sooner than I wanted. Oddly again, this is in the past as almost another year had gone by already since that day.

Atticus and I are seventeen and little Alaina was just months over being two. They grow up so fast are the right words. Seeming yesterday she was a crying baby and she can walk and talk as much for her age, probably even better. Her first word was daddy and later learned our names. She has a pretty decent vocabulary of words she can speak. Walking had improved with practice and she walks without falling. Thank you the crying had stopped. I envy parents whose children sleep all through the night and I am not even an actual parent.

When she grows much older than this it will difficult and emotional to explain this when she will ask about it. With all the why questions we get, I have my money put on it. That was not what we should be worried about. The time was January and for the past three or so years we have escaped the grasp of the illnesses that strikes the prison. I feared for Alaina for being young and not being able to hold out as in her still developing immune system. I was worried about the wrong person.

One morning about a week into the New Year I woke with violent cough and a sore throat. Not only that I felt like I was going to die and be miserable. My throat felt like it was on fire and soon made wretched sounds. My cough woke anyone who was around me which lucky for me were people I knew. As if the cough was an alarm clock they rose to find the snooze button hoping to find sleep in the next few minutes. I was still coughing when they looked toward me and it almost looked as if I was choking. Quickly noticing my distress my father got up and patted my back.

"Breath Mallca," my father commanded. It was really a request and eventually I did stop, "You okay?"

I nodded as I was unable to speak due to the cough and throat. Slowly I breathed in and out through both my nose and mouth. I was so tired even after going to bed early last night. It was unlike me to go to bed as soon as we're able to return to the barrack and I apologized to my father about him having to take care of Alaina again. Atticus was kind enough to watch her too. On the fact of turning in early they swore something was wrong with me. I too swore something was wrong with me as I can be called a night owl, but I make to sleep at night. Going back to sleep seemed like the best idea I could have all-day. That was not going to be an option because a screeching siren would be the wakeup call in ten minutes. I could sleep through breakfast, but that would not have been a smart in keeping my strength up.

I was exhausted and just want this day to go by in a blink of an eye so I could sleep. Hopefully I would be feeling better in the morning. I did not understand why I would be this tired; I have not over worked myself and behaved. As I began to doze off to somewhere the alarm went off. The sound rang normally, but felt so loud in my ears like my hearing was enhanced. I sat up hopefully to clear my head of this feeling to have someone grab my arm pulling up. Whoever did it I wished they had not of pulled me.

Dizziness washed over me leaving me light headed and vomiting felt like an option right then. I decided to fight it and get through the day. I felt I was strong enough to fight this bug off so I could just rest later. My stubbornness would get me in trouble as I did not even last until lunch.

Going out the barrack door in the morning sun after breakfast, which I had barely touched except for meaningless bites, my eyes squinted and became in pain to the brightness. It wasn't all that was bright yet, but it felt like the sun skipped to high noon. The sun revealed that it had been Atticus who had pulled me. As we came into the light Atticus could clearly see that my face had bluish pale coloration.

"Mallca, are you sure you are okay? We don't need you to pass out or something," he asked.

"Yes, I'm fine," I replied revealing that there was hoariness in my voice. Both Atticus and I were shocked by this fact, before either could comment on my voice a guard yelled at us to get to work.

"Please do not overdo it," he whispered as we began to start our daily routine. I simply nodded, but I made no promises. Also when do I ever do what I am told?

As we began to work I instantly became sore and cold all over my body. Chills ran up and down freezing different places remaining that way. My body was stiff and with a simple shove I could have collapsed. The weight I carried seemed to weigh a ton like bricks. With a glance I looked down at my cargo in hand to see a red liquid on the top. I felt something wet on my nose, but I assumed my nose was only bleeding from a simple nose bleed from it being dry or something along natural bleeds.

"Pick up the pace!" I heard in the distance. I could not comply with his command as much as I did not want to. In a wave everything I had been feeling that day and additions to that hit my weak body. I thought I had come from a torture chamber three days ago just barely making it out alive.

My breathing became labored and rapid like as I ran marathon and having an asthma attack. This caused my throat to become sorer, worse than that morning. Trying to gasp for air I was coughing up more than I could take in. I could tell I was having trouble swallowing the saliva because it was painful. All the gasping and needing air made coughing fits sounds of croup-like or barking. To keep my germs from spread to the people coming closer I covered my mouth. If someone was to try to offer water I wouldn't be able to talk. Knowing this cough I would just spit it back out. I knew my hand covering my mouth would feel wet from what I thought was spit. When I removed my hand after the coughing subsided I saw blood. Where was this coming from? It was from both my mouth and nose plus the coughing brought it up from lungs which only hoped drained from my nose. Atticus heard me from his position, he didn't notice at first as no one did, and turned to see me on the ground during my whole fit.

"Mallca!" he cried out dropping his load on the ground and running toward me. Besides Attiscus and the none sadist people around me, the others just watched as I was practically dying from who knows what. Maurus came running up moments later hearing the commotion. At the moment I laid still as if I was frozen.

"Help me get her back to your barrack," Maurus said to Atticus. Maurus picked me up bridal style carrying me with Atticus on his heels.

I was both cold and hot. My inside burned with a fever while my outside froze from the weather. From there, my condition only got worse. My abdomen was scrunched and I began to cough again. I buried my face in my right shoulder to keep from spreading whatever I had to Maurus who was the only person who really helps us and takes the risk of getting caught. Again I spit up blood which combine with a drool that leaked on my shoulder. With the clearness that I had in my head I thought it was gross. When we eventually reached the barrack my coughing subsided.

"Is she going to be okay?" Atticus asked. Maurus gently laid me on my cot and placed the back of his hand on my forehead before answering.

"She's burning up . . ." he replied with shakiness in his voice.

"But is she going to be okay?" he asked again. It was a simple yes or no question that anyone could basically answer if they knew what they were doing. Anyone could tell Maurus was avoiding the question. "Tell me."

"I don't know. It could be what people get every year around here, but I do not remember the name," he answered. He sounded like he actually cared about what happens to any of us. "We don't have a doctor here so I can't tell."

As those words left his mouth Atticus suddenly acquired an idea, he was already studying to become what they needed. In the class about doctoring he was already studying diseases and their symptoms. All the ones I was experiencing seemed familiar to him. In his head he listed them: fever, sore throat, chills, hoarseness, bluish coloration, blood draining, painful swallowing, and breathing problems. The only symptoms missing were skin lesions and . . . drooling. He saw on my shoulder what had come out if my mouth earlier. He was pretty sure that his idea about what I had contracted was . . . diphtheria.

"I think she has diphtheria . . ." Atticus suggested in painful voice. Maurus had the look of despair written across it. Hearing that name he knew that was the disease that he could not remember the name.

"We've had a couple cases each year and none of the breakers have survived. When a guard catches it we have medicine, but I am not sure what it's called," Maurus explained.

"We would need penicillin," he explained. Atticus was grateful that he had paid attention during class when the teacher had spoken of diphtheria. If not I could of just laid here on this cot dying of an unknown illness that no one could remember the name of.

"I think they have that in our barrack in the medicine locker, but that is for authorized personal only. They only use it for guards though and I am unable to access it," Maurus stated.

"I am not just going to sit by her and allow her to die," Atticus snapped in a strong tone; he was as serious as a heart attack. Maurus could tell that emotion ruled over anything in this case.

However, that does not cure diseases that people die from. Atticus then said something afterwards that told Maurus that this boy really cared for me. "Where is it?"

"What?" he asked.

"The medical locker that has the penicillin," Atticus answered. He was no longer messing around.

"You're crazy to go and get it. If you're caught who knows what punishment you'll get or worse, death," Maurus explained.

The white building was where everyone only dared to approach unaccompanied by a guard. They had comfy beds, decent meals that were better than are own, and could mostly be seen like home. Basically in there was paradise compared to the hell we endured in our own barracks.

"I don't care. All I am asking is for to get me in there and pass security so I can grab the medicine she needs," Atticus pleaded. In his eyes and tone he was in desperate need of help.

Maurus wasn't sure what to do with helping Atticus. If he helped Atticus he risked the chance of getting caught. That would mean he would become a prisoner himself or just put to death. The other option if not helping him would lead to the horrible outcomes of either Atticus getting himself killed getting the medicine, or my own death. The way it looked either way it was possible that someone could die.

Anyone who had seen me earlier and that looked down at me could see I was much paler then when I was brought in. My condition was disintegrating at an alarming rate. The blood had already dried on my clothes as another stain that isn't going to come out. By the condition state of my disease it could be said I had been sick for a couple days or the weakness of my current body made it hit worse than average. I could have had the symptoms without knowing it and showing any signs. This would have given the time for the diphtheria to set into my system and attack; it was slowly killing me from the inside to revealing itself on the outside for people to know. The only two people who actually knew of my illness thought it could not get any worse for me.

"What are those on her arm?" Maurus asked getting a final look at me before telling Atticus his decision. Atticus turned to look to at me to see red spots on my arm. They were only minor, but if not dealt with, they could only get worse. He had his suspicious, and they were proven to be correct if my condition was indeed diphtheria. Atticus eyes were distressed and the spots looked painful. If he did not do something to aid me I would die an excruciating death.

"They're lesions," he answered, "the diphtheria is getting worse for every minute we wait, so please?"

Maurus nodded knowing that he was taking a gigantic risk by helping Atticus. He helped us because he saw that we were the people that were not afraid to fight for what he believed in too. He would pass Atticus for what he actually was, a breaker, and slip inside as Maurus bringing him to report to Batson about him. The only one speaking to Batson would be Maurus and Atticus would never face him.

They had no time to waste or it could too late as my illness could kill me or severely damage my organs leaving life changing issues like nerve damage such as paralysis or the flow of blood that pumps to my heart. My motionless body just laid on the cot all alone and it would stay that way. Maurus asked that no one come near as I could infect everyone around me. Even if this was not contagious I would not allow my family to come near me for their own sake. For Alaina that would be most likely fatal.

"Mallca okay?" Alaina asked in an innocent child voice, because that was all she was. We had told her that big brother Vaughan had left and she would see him one day. My father said he would explain it later to her. He did not want to lie to her, but telling her the truth would only cause worry and the urge to come and see me. He was already worried for my health and she did not need to be running in to see me. Her seeing me in this state would be terrifying and lead to the higher chance of infection. I learned that child under the age of five or adults over the age of forty have higher fatality percent of dying. Both of the two remaining Siyas, besides myself, were in that age range and probably would not survive.

"She's fine. Mallca is just getting some rest," our father lied. He winced inside that he had to do that to her.

"I see her?" she asked.

"No, I'm sorry honey. Mallca probably should be left alone," he explained.

"Why?" she asked. The infamous question asked by a two year old.

"She doesn't want to be disturbed and you could wake her up," he tried to reason with her.

"I won't," she pleaded.

"No," my father said strictly hoping to get the point across, hoping not to sound to mean like he has done with me in the past.

"Daddy!" she whined, "Why?"

"Because she's sick!" my father snapped revealing the truth with tears starting to build in his eyes. Alaina also not understanding why her father had yelled began to sob. Quickly he scooped her up in his arms silencing her crying. He could not lose another child again.

Maurus dragged Atticus by the arm toward the white barrack. It was not rough, just enough that it looked real to convince people. As they crossed the grounds people eyes wondered at what Atticus had done and that it was usually me that was being dragged. The thought of him doing something rash for me was acceptable in their eyes. As they approached the building two guards stepped out to meet them.

"What's this?" one asked.

"I need to speak with Batson in regards of this one and other matters concerning a couple of breakers," Maurus explained with a straight face. The guards nodded and opened the doors. Walking down the halls no one was in sight to see them. If they received any suspicious looks, they were ignored. Outside Batson's office Maurus released Atticus and looked around.

"Go down the hall to the right and it is the first door on the right. The medical room is there and the penicillin should in the cabinet. I'll distract Batson long enough to give you the time," Maurus explained in a whisper to where he voice would not travel through the doors alerting Batson. Atticus nodded leaving and Maurus knocked on the door.

"Enter!" yelled that strong rough voice said from the other side. Maurus entered to see Batson sitting at his desk smoking a cigar. "What?"

"I thought I should inform you that we have our first case of diphtheria today," Maurus said.

"Really, came early this year. Whose symbol?" he asked blowing out a smoke of grey cigar smoke.

"The wyvern," Maurus answered with only little hesitation about the answer.

Batson chuckled at the thought that the wyvern was taken was taken down to a dying body by diphtheria. He thought that it would have probably been him to finally put me in my place and he hoped it to be so. Maurus had a different idea. If Batson was not in his place of power and it would not either cost him his life or mine he would of defended me. Probably he thought about just telling him off or something. I would have actually done it.

Atticus quietly traveled down the hall to the medical room where Maurus said it was. Something about Maurus never sat right with Atticus and he had less trust in him than I did. For all he knew he could have sent him to the guard's quarters to turn him in. The fact that he was helping him gave him some trust in him.

Atticus would know if he could trust him if this planned out to successful. Lucky he was sent to the right room and no one was there. Looking around the room after setting sights on the cabinet he went straight to it. Looking inside Atticus thought who ever stocked this had to have OCD like myself. Yes, I have OCD, but that is not the point. Atticus easily found the penicillin at the middle to bottom. Also in the cabinet were syringes and that was the only way, with the penicillin at hand, could be dispensed. Just as he had it safely in his hand he heard footsteps coming in his direction. Quickly in one slide Atticus dove under the bed hoping he would not be discovered.

"Atticus . . ." a voice whispered into the room. Atticus recognized the voice belonging to Maurus. Looking he made sure it was clear for him to emerge from hiding. "Did you get it?" Atticus answered by showing him the bottle. Before leaving the medical room Maurus grabbed another bottle off the top shelf with a second syringe and as before they quickly made their way out without being spotted by anyone. Atticus did not question his actions hoping he had his reasons.

When they arrived back at the barrack neither of them liked what they saw about my condition as I was lying on the cot with the palest face. A better way to view it is that someone took white make-up and applied it to my face so that I looked dead. Slowly Atticus touched my neck and it was cold. Placing two fingers upon my neck he was relieved to feel a pulse, but it was faintly failing. That could only mean I was running out of time.

"If we do not administer the penicillin now she may not survive," Maurus pointed the obvious that Atticus already knew. Atticus looked down at the medicine and syringe in his hands not knowing what to think. He then handed the supplies to Maurus.

"I can't do it . . ." he mumbled. Maurus nodded knowing that if he were in Atticus's place he could not inject me with all that could help me either. The fact that something could happen to me afterward could end in telling Atticus that it was his fault. Simply the life he was in love with would be in his hands.

Maurus then leaned down touching my cold arm and got no reaction to his warm touch. He even tried calling my name to still receive no response. Neither did the verbal or pain stimulus even attempt to arouse me. With his now cooled hand he reached to my forehead to feel the temperature of my fever. My fever was low and normally that is a significant improvement, but not in this case.

"Before I do this, do you know if she is allergic to the medication?" Maurus asked. He needed to be sure before giving it to me. If so the reaction could kill me first before the illness does.

"I don't know," Atticus answered. Maurus just added another fear to Atticus's list. The other two were that I was afraid of needles and that it could be late. With needles I would always have a panic attack and it would take serious convincing to allow the nurse to stick me. I'm not kidding, my aunt had to sit on me one time when I had to get them for school one year.

"You are aware of that I do not know if she will react to the penicillin so this is dangerous to attempt. Where is Mr. Siyas? He should know right?" Maurus asked.

"I don't know where he went. Maybe he took Alaina out or something. Should I go and try to find him?" Atticus asked. Maurus thought about it and returned to the look at me. He did not believe they had the time to waste waiting.

"No. We will just have to hope that she is not and she won't wake up so we can't ask her," Maurus said. Atticus then saw Maurus curse under his breath.

"Okay," Atticus said. Maurus nodded and prayed.

Carefully he began to take out the penicillin with the syringe from the glass bottle. Atticus did not want to watch as Maurus placed the needle into my arm. Every fiber inside him wanted to either turn away or close his eyes, but he just couldn't. I did not even flinch or have any reaction to the needle as I was told. Actually I did not even feel it go into my arm or anything at all. Was that a good sign or not?

"Is she going to be alright?" Atticus asked very concerned about what all had occurred and what still could.

I felt so weird and I wasn't sure what was going and Atticus got his answer moments later as my skin became red in patches; hives were occurring on my skin. I was itchy and could stop as I began to become sicker. Also it sounded as if I was choking on air and my head tilted side to side as if I were dizzy. Upon seeing this Maurus quickly placed his hand on my neck. My pulse was weaker than it was before. Slowly I grew weaker and could eventually die.

"Dammit! She is having a reaction!" Maurus cried out. Suddenly he grabbed the bottle he took out and other syringe taking amount an acceptable amount. Quickly aiming correctly he jabbed that into my arm. Slowly the allergic reaction calmed.

"What was that?!" Atticus exclaimed still in the shock of what he was just in witnessed to.

"Epinephrine," Maurus answered. Atticus looked confused at the medical word he had yet learned. "Adrenaline, it helps calm down the anaphylaxis reaction. I thought this may occur so I grabbed a bottle just in case and I am glad I did. As long as we watch her she should be alright."

"Should be?" Atticus asked.

"When I return in the morning I will grab some diphenhydramine and rifampin and bring it to her. Those should help with the illness then the reaction," he explained.

"How do you know all this?" Atticus asked. He had wondered how he knew all this information and he believed he was just a guard.

"In my own Predetermine I had to learn to be a medic then I was to be interrupted and have a career change to a guard," Maurus explained.

"I'm sorry to hear that," Atticus replied.

"It's okay. Now I can help people here, like you, and hoping they'll get out safely."

Only time would tell if I would survive either the allergic reaction or the diphtheria or not. Would the penicillin still work or cancel out? Maurus had told Atticus was bringing something else which was to used as a substitute. So many questions of my condition and the outcomes just kept going. Would I be the next in my family to die?

To be honest, Atticus should not be worried about the diphtheria and if I will live or not. Even in the prison they expect breakers to keep following both their rules and live up to their own Predetermine. Oddly our Predetermines were now coming true. I was sick and dying and Atticus could be losing his possible spouse. If the problem cannot be seen already it is by not following out the Predetermine you die. Their world has no room for people who can not live out what they were destined for. Destined? More like subjucted to by threats. I may already be dead, Atticus isn't and we aren't married. Basically if I die, so does Atticus if we are Predetermined.

Chapter

9

Atticus sat with me the entire night, of that I could tell. It was just that feeling of a presence there. I wasn't awake, but I could feel him there next to me. It's hard to explain. Maurus warned Atticus that he should stay away because of the risk of getting sick, but Atticus is stubborn. Also he informed Maurus that before high school his over protective mother made him get a vaccine that protects him from these kinds of illnesses. That was of lucky him, but not so much for me. Other than that I did not feel like I was getting any better and I surely did not look like it.

I was still pale in the face and cold to the touch. My fever was at least lower, but I still was warm. Because of my reaction to the penicillin I was having trouble breathing and every once in a while wheezing could be heard. However, most my other injuries were healing like the lesions. They were wrapped to prevent infection because that was all I needed. Maurus did come the next day and given me an antihistamine. That helped with my hives and breathing.

"Is she getting any better?" Atticus came in and asked during the mid-day break.

"It's hard to tell until she wakes up," Maurus said taking a glance over at me, "looking at her physically it does not look good, but I could be wrong."

"I know and if she doesn't survive it could affect me," Atticus admitted.

"Why is that?" Maurus asked.

"Both Mallca's and my own Predetermine are somehow linked to each other by being similar. I believe it means she is the one I am supposed to marry," Atticus explained.

Upon hearing this Maurus wondered if Atticus knew about the rule here. If the individual cannot complete his or her Predetermine; they will die. I guess this was another way to convince people not to break theirs. Maurus asked Atticus this question and Atticus's face dropped. Only two ways could fix this problem: for me to survive or to marry me.

"I think I know someone who can help you. Hold on, I'll be back," Maurus said leaving to go find someone. Atticus had the job to find my father because we were under the age of eighteen.

After work had been completed that day Atticus found my father sitting with Alaina at the front of the barrack. It was quiet without me there. I was in the back of the barrack fighting for my life. If I was better I would be keeping Alaina company and out of trouble. It had been a while since my father had to take care of children since his two had grown up, but it seemed it was like riding a bike. Especially since the last time was about when Vaughan was a little kid and I became the responsible one . . . 'right', which was what my parents thought.

"Mr. Siyas?" Atticus asked walking up to get my father's attention and ended up scaring him. Atticus raised his hands showing him no harm.

"Yes Atticus?" my father acknowledged him.

"I have a very important question to ask you. I completely understand if you decline because it will change all known between our families . . ." Atticus started.

"Just say it," my father said. Just like me; get to the point of what you're going to say or ask and no fluff.

"May I have your blessing to marry Mallca in order to save our lives?" Atticus asked, "I know I maybe sounding selfish in saving myself, but I see it as saving us both."

My father looked dumbfounded and lost for words. Well it was better than saying I had just died in my sleep. My father wanted to keep the conversation going, but the question why was answered; he wanted to save me. All he could do was nod as a glint of sadness entered his eyes. He oldest daughter was going to be forced into marriage to save lives and it wasn't just that. This was a day he looked forward to his entire life with children. He wanted to be able to walk me down the aisle and hand me off to the love of my life who he hoped would be Atticus. My father liked Atticus and I had to marry someone he would want him to be my husband. He didn't want to see me wed in this dump of a place on my death bed, but in a beautiful church wearing mom's white dress. Worse part of it all was that his wife wasn't here to see. He nodded. Atticus whispered a thank you before going to find Maurus. He found him in the back with another man.

"Who's this?" he asked. The man looked to be in his fifties and completely innocent like everyone else in here. No one could have guessed that he had done anything wrong to deserve to be placed in here.

"This is Riender. He's a priest," Maurus introduced him.

"I broke my Predetermine by wanting to and marrying a church girl when I suppose to be alone," Riender explained without being asked the question people knew was often asked. "I know most people ask so that's why I answered ahead or I just knew you were thinking it."

Atticus tilted his head back as a sign of he understood. Not to mention that Riender was right about thinking the question. I found it terrible when The Committee gives a Predetermine you cannot help but break because of how it was made. Who could only just stand there and watch it all disappear?

"He is certified to marry you. Did you ask her father?" Maurus asked.

"Yes," Atticus answered.

"Then let us begin . . ." Riender started.

"Wait!" Maurus interrupted holding out two silver nuts, "I took these from one of the machines. They should work as rings." Atticus thanked Maurus and returned to my side with Riender at the other.

"I'm going to make this quick. Do you, Atticus Issigna, take Mallca Siyas to be your wife? To love, hold, to care for in sickness and in health . . ." Riender started.

"I do." That was all Atticus had to say and never once did he have second thoughts.

Riender looked down to me wondering if he should go on or not with my condition. With me being at risk of dying and being unconscious at the moment didn't say much that I wanted this as much as Atticus did.

"Is there anyone here to speak for her on her behalf? If not I have to cancel the matrimony," Riender explained.

Both younger men looked at each other worried. Atticus being the one going to be married to me could not speak and Maurus hasn't known me long enough to know. Plus the fact hardly anyone knows how I feel about anything. Atticus thought asking my father was enough and thought it best not to bring this on to him, but he was all that was left. Slowly Atticus hopes began to die with the fact that both of us were probably going to die. Hope began to both die and increase as footsteps were heard behind him. It could have been a hopeful soul or a guard.

"I know she'll agree to it. I can tell that she loves you as much as her family, but she's just too stubborn to admit it," my father said coming behind them. Before going to my side to hold my hand he placed his hand on Atticus's shoulder giving it a comforting squeeze telling him he was happy.

"Thank you," Atticus replied even tearing up a little.

"Well then if the father of the bride agrees to the matrimony of these two, I now pronounce you husband and wife," Riender finished smiling hoping he had done the right action.

Atticus held my hand tighter; he was afraid to kiss me. He may be protected from the illness, but that didn't mean much. With direct contact could increase the chances of him getting sick or me even waking up. Whichever way that occurred was a worst case scenario because Atticus would probably die. Instead he placed one of the nuts on my left ring finger and kissed me on the forehead. I guess a kiss there is better than none at all in his eyes. However, last he checked up on me my fever was slowly frying my brain, but it did not seem that way.

"I think her fever's gone," Atticus said after feeling my forehead. Maurus quickly got between us and placed his hand on my forehead and two fingers on my neck.

"I think he's right; her pulse is stronger and the fever has deceased," Maurus assured.

Everyone's faces were in relief that my condition was improving. My father did not have to worry about one of his daughters like he did his son. The fact my fever dropped from like 102 degrees was reassuring. True the paleness in my face and the sweat that made my hair looked like I had just taken a hot shower or came out of a sauna didn't help, but the fact I was not dying anymore made my appearance excusable. One aspect that did not change was they would still be playing the waiting game. It was never fun to play and objective depended on the key player, me, and I needed to wake up. I don't know how long Atticus had been sitting there next me. Oddly I knew he was there like earlier. It seemed like the time felt as three o'clock in the morning when I felt alive for the first time ever since falling ill.

"Mallca, if you can hear me," I heard a male voice say and I could decipher that it was Atticus, "I need you to wake. Please say something. I don't want to lose you."

The feeling of conciseness came and even with my eyes closed I began to feel awake. I was simply just resting my eyes. It felt good not to be as sick as I was and just feeling tired. However, most aspects about people never change; if I was dead, dying, or alive Atticus left me an opening to be a smartass.

"... Some ... thing ..." I whispered in a barely audible voice. I was lucky to be heard and I was.

"Mallca ..." Atticus cooed grabbing my hand and I could feel his tears drop down on my hand. He leaned in as I tried to get up and hugged me. I was tired of resting and wanted to get up. I had about ... I don't really know how many days I have been out, but I know it has been more than two days of rest and that seemed like enough. Atticus then released me and the unexpected happened. I expected him to say some comforting and full of emotional words. Out of nowhere Atticus kissed me right on the lips. I did have to admit that he was a good kisser, although it was sloppy on both ends, but being surprised by the action caused me push away.

'What the hell?' I thought and should have said, but Atticus realized what he just did.

"I'm so sorry," he apologized, "I just was afraid that you were going to die so ..."

I was speechless and I understood every word that he said, even if he didn't even say it. Atticus Issigna said that he loved me. I had always suspected, but never proven true. Something felt different though, besides the feelings toward Atticus. It felt as if something was on my finger. Then I looked down at my finger to the silver nut; I had an idea.

"Are...we?" I asked nervously in a sort of stutter.

"Married?" he finished, "Yes. I understand if you don't want to continue on, but our Predetermines would kill us if either you died or something ..."

Atticus just kept mumbling and I listened to what he had to say. He babbles when he's nervous and it is kind of cute. Just another trait to like about him I guess. I did not answer just letting it all sink in. I was seventeen years old, married to my best friend who I kind of had a crush on, and he asked me how I feel about it? Well I don't know what to think, but every girl that ever liked him would be so jealous. Most people actually could say they saw it coming, but we both denied it. However, I had one request.

"I didn't say I did not like it, but I get to keep my last name and I will just add yours on to it," I replied placing my tired head on his shoulder. I could just drift away. Then I noticed something else about what just occurred; I got my first kiss and it was by Atticus Issigna.

"You know your my first right?" I informed looking up into his eyes. For the first time in a long time I felt like I saw the sky.

"Me too," he replied beginning to stroke my hair.

That was something I thought I knew, but was not sure. I never asked Atticus, but I was sure he had at least had one girlfriend that he kept secret from me thinking I could intimidate her. With her and time he could have at least had one kiss. I feel special and have another reason to get better. Looking from Atticus shoulder I saw my father smiling. He looked happy that I was alright and happy for me. Alaina was beside him with the biggest grin I had ever seen her give. She was overjoyed to see me alive and somewhat well. Right now nothing could have ruined this moment.

Pain up though the body and inside the heart so suddenly. It would not stop and all this happened in front of my eyes. What was wrong with you? Your eyes are widening with pain. You were fine a second ago even smiling at me?!

"Dad!" I cried out while watching him fall and trying to get up to go to him. My body was still weak and fights my moments. Both my father and I collapse at the same time.

"Mallca!" I hear from Atticus, "Mr. Siyas!"

Atticus quickly laid me back down on the back down and ran to grab Alaina, succeeding in getting her away from the occurring scene, as Maurus went to my father. He was on the floor, hardly moving, and it barely seemed as if he was breathing.

"Daddy?" Alaina asked hoping to get some response. She tried to get past Atticus's arms to see what was going on. She was so scared and this happened so sudden. Already she had lost a mother who she'll never know, a brother she hardly knew, and almost a sister that is her biggest fan and vice versa. I know Alaina thinks the world of my father and me. Life was just not fair.

"Can you tell Mallca to take care of herself and Alaina . . . I love them both so much," my father, Arrington Siyas, said as he grasped Maurus's hand to stay with them for even just a little longer. Maurus nodded to assure him that he would let me know.

He had seen this all before with all different families like mine.

All the labor and sorrow of losing all the love ones in such little amount of time takes a toll. Causing the heart to give out and stop.

It can be explained as he had a heart attack. That is actually what happened to my father in more ways than one. There on the cold floor beside me, being a lifeless soul, my dad died next to me. It was like déjà vu.

Oblivious to what actually happened early that day I woke with a scare. Not sure if it was a nightmare or did I see something I should not have before I passed out. I opened my eyes to see Alaina next to me sleeping soundly in the crook of my arm. Her face was buried down in my shoulder like she was trying to hide from something. Gently I caressed her brown blonde hair and as my hand came through with the first stroke she awoke. Her eyes were red. *Had she been crying?*

"What's wrong?" I asked softly from my tiredness.

"Atty said daddy sleep," Alaina answered.

"Oh, let him sleep then, he needs it." I didn't know what she meant by this.

"No, daddy not wake up."

At the moment I was really dense and tired, but she was only a child. She was told what was easier to understand which for her it was hard because she was pretty smart and so far all of her childhood is in this place.

"Mallca . . ." Atticus said. I could hear the sadness in his voice.

I was not going to like what he was about to say and would he just get it over with. "Your father died a couple hours ago. I'm sorry to have to tell you."

My eyes widen as tears instantly came to my eyes and I finally begin to understand what was going on. I wanted someone to cry upon and there was no one around. Atticus kept his distance away afraid I could snap, but that was not what I wanted. Maurus stood there and watched. I agree with him that it would too weird if he had been the one to comfort me. Alaina being the last one wrapped her arms around side and leaned in close. Slowly I tilted my head back on the uncomfortable pillow.

"Mall . . ." Atticus started before an ear ringing screech interrupted him that originated from my mouth. I wanted to lash out, but I had to protect Alaina. She was the only one left of my family that would come in contact with me and lashing out would only put her at risk. That's all I needed was her being afraid of me. I kept wondering what would happen. I got my answer when the door suddenly flew open and three guards came marching toward us.

"By the ruling of President Illingsworth, Alaina Kenari Siyas, is to be taken into social service custody," said the guard in the middle with demanding voice. The two remaining guards came over our way. Maurus could only stand by and watch.

"It would be in your best interest not to interfere with our mission," said the second guard. A loud scream erupted in my head; it was my baby sister being pulled from my arms.

"Mallca!" she screamed for me to come and rescue her. I tiredly and weakly tried to get up and pursue her captors. It all went down as I got to my feet. My body fell forward hitting the solid cold concrete and began to blackout. The last image was blurry, but I saw Alaina being taken away. The last of my blood family was gone and I thought I would never see them again.

Chapter

10

It all almost seemed pointless; I had no reason to bother to continue on. That was not the case even though, it was how I felt. In reality that was not true. I had something to fight for and she was only two years old. Through all the whippings I later endured and other means of punishment they could inflict I would never give up. All I wanted was out of this retched hell of a place. Anything was better than here, maybe even death. Sometimes I wished I had died. When I was whipped, I could have bled to death or when I contracted diphtheria that winter. That would only make future events more difficult to handle. It seemed like we were never going to get out of here.

It seemed like a regular day in mid-June when we were called out for a discussion of some sort. Who knows what these people want these days? Only the people who work here would know what was going on. Lucky that I knew someone who worked here that could tell me what I wanted to know.

"What's going on here?" I asked Maurus who was among the crowd keeping them under control. He actually had a glimmer of hope residing in his eyes. What happiness could be given here?

"People have served their time," Maurus answered. Both mine and Atticus's face disarrayed showing we did not know what he meant by that. "People are being released."

My heart felt like it jumped with emotions such as joy, but also fear all colliding at the same time creating this combined emotion. I did not know what to think. If only my father could have stayed strong for a little longer. He could have gone free and Alaina still maybe here among us. With him being released she would have gone with him even if I didn't. He said people though. That did not mean everyone was being released. Like I said with my father I hoped Atticus would be released even if I was not so lucky. Considering my actions that have occurred since my arrival a little over three years ago to basically being a pain in the ass all this time it was pretty good assumption that I would not be leaving anytime soon. The question was why we had not gone through this before. Perhaps it was that they had such a small amount of people so why release them? Why not keep them just a little longer to make sure they learned their lesson? It wasn't like anyone would find out. I found out the truth.

"We shall call out your imprint and you shall step forward . . . mouse!" Batson called. A young girl roughly fifteen stepped out with blonde hair more scarred than anyone else here. I wondered what she did to deserve to be sent here. Probably something simple that can be simply overlooked after one to two years.

"Clock!"

"Dog!"

The animals and objects went on with people that I did not know. Some of the people looked familiar, but not anyone who I had any connections with. Well, the only connections I had here were with people I came with or Maurus. I have had a couple close calls, but somehow I pushed them away. Considering all that has happened with and around me I would not blame them. I would not have blamed Atticus if he had decided to dump me and leave, but was it like he hasd a choice. Finally I heard a symbol that I did not know until the owner appeared at my side.

"Owl!"

I looked around to see no one step forward to claim the mark. I felt a gentle hand touch my shoulder. I turned to see who it was and I met a familiar pair of lips meet mine. It was Atticus.

"It's going to be okay. I know it will," he said as he released my lips from his clasp and walked forward to join the rest of the crowd who all waited to be released.

I could not believe it. For starters I was relieved that Atticus was getting out of here. At least I would not have to worry about him leaving me for good. That would be all I needed. Second, with three years, more or less, since the pain of being branded I never knew what his mark was. To be fair he doesn't know what mine is either. From what I know of owls it is weird because they fit together. Like of marks mean something about ourselves.

Atticus may not see it, but he sees through people or at least the mask they have decided to hide under. When we were kids, before I knew Atticus, I use to pretend I was a cool kid, but Atticus broke me and I became myself. He has patience for when he waited for me to realize that I was in love with him. Not only that, him watching over me and helping me when I sick. Maybe those are some of the qualities that I see in him as the guy I am in love with. When I actually got to see his mark I noticed that it was fierce looking bird ready to strike down and take out those who challenged it. Even with the savage appearance it still had that tranquil and assertive look. That seems to describe Atticus to the letter.

I waited patiently as the rest of the breakers were being called to receive freedom. Already about thirty people were called and not many seemed left to be called. It was the feeling that the list was just getting shorter until it ends with my chances getting slimmer. As time went on I noticed before another was called I noticed something had changed in Batson's body language. He seemed not wanting to continue on with the list. The man swallowed what seemed to be the last of his pride I had left him before speaking again.

"Wyvern," he said.

I let out a sigh of relief and I thanked what blessings I had left. This nightmare was over, but that did not mean more would come. Finally I was away from the atrocious man that took the pleasure in beating me and watching me suffer. I was glad the last sight of him was the way similar when I stood up to him all those times. This made me light-hearted.

As I walked toward the crowd I looked around to see the people who were left just glaring at me, watching me be on my way to the outside. They were burning in. What did I do to deserve this? As I was aware I did nothing to them; if anyone should be angry it should be Batson or at least be angry with him. Unless I made life miserable here on because of my actions and if that was the case I was sorry. Inside they are delighted to see me go.

The ride back could be described as luxurious compared to the ride going into the prison. First of all the weather was much nicer besides the heat, but the fact our clothes were worn out gave the rushing air room to enter thus cooling us down. Like an air conditioner or the truth, sitting in the back of a truck letting the air come across the skin. The heat made everyone sweat and all the air did for that was dry it. I was going to need like a day shower because the only shower you got in hell was when you worked in the pouring rain. Jokingly, that wasn't very often as it was too hot to rain in hell. I made sure I sat next to Atticus. No one had any burns on their arm that had a risk of getting infected. The position of staying alive and strong was not their way to keep the mind at ease and awake. Boredom however sat in as there was not much to talk about. No one would speak about what they planned to do when they returned to civilization. I knew what I was going to do; find Alaina and take her back to where she belongs, with me.

Eventually I scooted closer to Atticus and placed my head on his shoulder. It was actually more comfortable then people could have thought. He then gently caressed my hair and caused, what that usually does, making me tired. I did not fight when sleep came to me next. The trip was what I really did not remember, but it was relatively peaceful and I believe we did not lose anyone. They had no reason to try and escape. They finally going toward that escape.

I thought it was nice that they returned us to our homes. I told Atticus that I would stop by later and allow him and Daphnia some time together. Also it gave sometime between all the news before we broke it to her that we were married. At least that is what I thought I did. When they dropped me at my home I was in shock. Atticus was overjoyed to be going home that he did not notice anything. Still, the house in front of me was not the one I left. Yes, the shape was familiar, but the color was different. It used to be a baby blue and now it was white. Also my family never owned either a sandbox or play set. Now I understand what happened, someone else had moved in. Since we left we still owned the house, but the owners, being my parents, died and I was not here to claim the house so they put it up on the market. Worst case scenario happened, the place I grew up was gone and someone bought it. I cried at the fact that all of my father's hard work was destroyed. The pond was in terrible condition and the yard was torn up from constant remodeling and play. I could see where the flowers had died. My only question was, where was I supposed to live?

I walked the short distance to Atticus's home to hopefully have some peace and be welcome. Nothing was wrong and it seemed peaceful. I almost didn't go inside. The feeling of me being a disturbance and bringing my problems into his house and during the time with his mother was unsettling.. The one person he has wanted to since the day he left her and minute he got out. Also she would need him more than ever since he was the only child she had left. I entered the house with the reasoning that Daphnia told me that I was welcomed to come in anytime like I lived there too and that fact that I married to her son. Sooner or later we would have to tell her what had happened.

Pitch darkness was my greeting into the Issigna house instead of a happy hello. No life seemed inside the house. Maybe they were both out as soon as he walked into the door. True, the blinds were closed and that was a reason for the darkness. However, with all my years of knowing Daphnia, she was not the type to enjoy the dark. There was always a light on unless it was bedtime. That would explain the high power bill, but she seemed to handle it. The other dark feeling I felt was that something was wrong. I mean it seemed like something terrible happened and I just walked straight into it. Being in the dark about this both eyesight and vibe was not acceptable. However, me not knowing if Daphnia changed the house's layout or not put me at risk of bumping or falling over and hurting myself.

With small sounds of creaking came with every step I made toward the window. Luckily the open door gave some light so I could make it safely to the window. Opening the curtains and blinds sent an impetuous ray of light into my eyes. Even dazed I swore I saw a foot so allowing my eyes to catch up to my sockets before flipping on the switch to bring the full visibility to the room. I hate it when I am right as the open blinds didn't just bring sight. The foot belonged to my husband. That sounded weird to say. Rushing to his side I saw he was on his knees still conscious and weeping.

"Atticus what's wrong?" I asked him in deep concern. He seemed to only mumble words, but they were hardly intelligible. "I can't understand you honey."

"She's . . . gone," he replied softly. I then helped him to the couch and allowed him to explain, "I came home and on the door there was a notice . . . and it said . . ." He barely started before quietly sobbing again. Slowly I took the paper in his hand that was crumbled up and read it:

NOTICE!!

We are sorry to inform you, Atticus Joseph Issigna, that your mother had gotten sick two years ago and she passed away early this year. She has placed in her will after learning the death of Bethany Joy Issigna that everything is to be given to you. Knowing that you were to be released later in the year we shall not take anything and leave it all as it is. Again, we are sorry for the lost.

The Committee

Reading this I felt that I could keel over on the floor too like Atticus probably did upon reading the notice the first time. Indeed the loss of Daphnia was a toll on both me and Atticus. She was Atticus's mother and she was like a second one to me and my in-law. I can see it in his eyes that he feels and has empathy for when the last of my family or even when my parents were taken. True he lost his father at a young age, but he had time to move on where I had no room to do. The only thing I knew that I could do was be there for him like he was for me.

For the next few days Atticus, nor I, were normal or at least ourselves which we considered normal. It was like the week he lost his dad. He just wanted to lie around and do nothing. He was depressed going through the grieving stages and wanted to be alone. I did my best not to let him push me away and keep up with the rest of life. It all seemed good and what could go wrong. Sometimes, I really needed to learn to shut up.

That July we both received another notice in the mail and this one was not as bad as the last, but still sad. It was from the educational department and it said we had to finish our last year of high school. Neither of us saw the point of going back because it was only for a year as we already missed somewhat of the other three. I thought we had escaped school by going to the prison, but I suppose not. We had missed nearly everything and what was there to learn if we had no idea what they were talking about. I figured they would just catch us up and it would be alright. I guess we did not have a choice. No one ever does. Not completing high school would lead to no diploma leads to no jobs or college and breaking our Predetermines once again. I would rather be an archeologist than return to that place for who knows how much longer this time. It just never ends.

The Monday of the third week of August my clock went off at six-thirty and I got up to see the sun barely coming up. Atticus and I had couldn't start with everyone else because they had to put us back into the system and find our records. The only upside to starting late was neither Atticus nor I had to go to school on our birthdays. We were eighteen and thus considered adults and idependants. We were just considered minors before so we had didn't have to go through foster or anything. I figured this was why Alaina was taken from me as I was seventeen and they wouldn't consider me her guardian.

I looked over to see Atticus still sleeping. That boy can sleep through almost anything. I then went to the drawer and picked out something simple; just a pair of jeans and a nice top. Not that the top mattered because I was going to throw a jacket over it anyway. The morning felt the same as the morning when we found out Vaughan's Predetermine. It was now seven o'clock so I went and got Atticus up. At first he was reluctant, but after pestering him about it he got up. I waited down stairs drinking a cup of hot tea and eating a bagel with butter. I am really tired, but I won't touch the coffee we have. Atticus does not drink coffee either, but oddly he likes the smell of it. He then grabbed his breakfast and we ate silently.

I was unable to say this to him, but I was filled with mixed emotions; the main one I was feeling was fear. The fear of returning to this 'safe place' and have the possibility of being treated as a criminal that people believe I was. Everyone having the wrong idea of us and being hated; making school just another living nightmare five days a week eight in the morning until three in the afternoon. Atticus would be my only friend as I was sure my old friends would not want to talk to me. Plus I wondered if any of my not as close as Atticus friends would remember me anyway. After the day ended I think I can tally this on worst days ever, but it is near the end of the list.

It was now twenty minutes later and the bus was about to come. Daphnia may have left everything to Atticus like the car, but neither of us had a license to drive it. I just hoped it was not Mrs. Stephen because she hated me for no apparent reason. Before we walked outside Atticus smiled and he expected one in return. I tried to find reason, but nothing came to mind. I was being too pessimistic to think that this could end in a good outcome. I had to force one to appear and it hardly looked real. The big long yellow bus then appeared outside and we went out before it left without us.

Casually we walked down the path to meet the bus. Lucky us the driver was not Mrs. Stephen, but some older guy. He did not look happy about doing this job. He slowly opened the door and waited with an impatient look. Atticus went first after I gave him the look of I was not ready to go on. I was going to take any time I could to stall. That was not a good idea as it led to a rude action. Going last only got me the feeling of the slammed door nipping my black backpack. I flinched with both hearing and feeling it. Atticus then turned to me giving me the 'it is going to be okay look'. I returned with the 'yeah right'.

Walking up those three steps maybe the hardest steps I may have had to take that day. walking up to see all those faces look at you. The faces of judgment, confusion, curiosity, and the list only continued to get longer. One after another we walked down the aisles to see the faces of my new fellow classmates; some of them even looked familiar if I would just increase the age of the people I use to know. I heard the whispers come from one to the other. Sadly I could not hear what they were saying. I questioned if I would want to know what was said? I was positive that it was about Atticus and me.

To our advantage we found an empty seat so the both of us could sit together. It would have probably ended badly if we didn't. However, just before we sat down the driver took off and then slammed on the breaks. The slam sent Atticus flying face first into the seat we were just about to sit in as I grabbed the seat in front of me and then jerked backwards to the floor. I open my eyes to look at the metal roof and a pain in my back from the supplies in my bag. Not only that I heard laughing. This was not funny as the possibility of one us being hurt was still at large.

"Sorry! It was a squirrel running across the road!" the driver called back.

'Squirrel my ass,' I thought to myself as the next thing I see is Atticus's hand out to help me up. I got a good look at his face to see that he was alright and wasn't injured. I was fine except it only just felt like I got whiplash. When I got up and looked toward the front I swore I saw the driver grin. Bastard did that on purpose to rough us up and give the other kids a good laugh to start their day.

"You okay?" Atticus asked as we were settled into our seat.

"Yes," I replied showing a small smile, "You?"

"I'll be fine. I just wish I could shut these people up," he whispered. I giggled at his comment as I was thinking the same thing.

The ride to school was quiet. I was under the impression that no one had anything to say to anyone that was not about us. Eventually conversations were made that were not about us and the bus filled with chatter. I thought that if anyone spoke to us it would turn into non kind-hearted conversations or would bring up sensitive subjects.

When we arrived at the school everyone was getting off like there was a fire and the front door was the only exit. Atticus attempted to get up and allow us to get off, but he then received a rough push from another boy. He then laughed in his face. Apparently in any school level it was a ritual to pick on the new kids if they didn't seem to meet standards. If it had been me he shoved, the boy would not have gotten off so lucky. I was positive I would have gone to the principal's office on the first day. Whoever he was would have walked off the bus toward the nurse's office with a bloody nose.

I wanted to hold Atticus's hand the entire time we were going inside, but I would be putting so much at risk like any chances we may have in surviving this final school year. Sadly, we had only three class together and what all the other times alone I believed to be vulnerable. I know, me, thinking this way. As we went to our separate classes our hands brushed across each other smoothly. I just wanted to take him with me and have beside me all day. I knew the principal would not allow that even if he didn't know our little secrets.

My first class of the day was history. When I walked into my class my body moved directly toward the back of the room, unfortunately there were people already people there. They looked like the people would just judge me and be weaker versions of Batson. We all remember what I had done to him. Well at least here I get sent home and not beat up. Considering my position right now it would not be my best idea. Finally I decided to take a seat on the middle left side end, away from everyone else.

"Alright class we have a new student starting here this year today. You can introduce yourself," the teacher known as Mr. Peterson said.

"I would rather not," I replied quietly.

"Alright then that is okay, everyone is shy, but that will change by the end of the year. Well this is Mrs. Mallca Siyas-Issigna," he said reading the name I had to put on the registration papers. I did not have a choice because I would be lying and if found out I would be in serious trouble. At the prison everything was finalized and we were legally married. "Well, it looks like they made a mistake. I'll change it and let the office know. Ha, thcy said you were married!"

"It's right," I said. I could not stand that I could be living a lie. I knew that I could not get away with it for too long. They all would find out sooner or later.

"Excuse me? You're married?" he asked.

"Yes. Is there a problem?" I said.

"No, I guess not," he replied remembering what kind of world we all lived in.

Well so far the worst idea today was to tell my entire history class that I was married. Everyone seemed to have nothing better to do because they listened in to our conversation. In seconds I was bombarded with questions about myself that I was in no hurry or comfortable to answer. The questions include who I was married to, when, why, and more who's.

"Alright, let's leave Mallca to answer those when she is ready and let us begin class," Mr. Peterson said saving me from having to reveal my secrets. I do not remember what we had learned that day, but I really did not want it to end. I was literally saved by the bell when it rang. At a fast pace I rushed out of the room and heading to my next class. Later I learned I should have stayed there if I could; my next class was gym.

One of the female teachers there had lent my clothes for gym until I could get my own. This way I could at least participate and get the credit for the day. She had informed me some teachers do not care if this is your first day as they will give you the grade of F for the day and make you make it up later. I found out that my teacher was one of those kinds and male. When I finally met him he reminded me of Batson in a non-horrific physical aspect. He was muscular and didn't really have all those other traits I wished not to remember.

"Today we are climbing the wall!" he informed sternly. I looked over to see a rock wall that went to roughly ten feet high or higher.

'Do they even allow those in school?' I thought. I could see students getting hurt. Well, as the thought of safety had crossed my mind I heard the scream of a girl who just failed and fell. She wasn't very high up and landed semi on her feet. I could not wait for my turn.

"New girl!" he shouted, "You're up!"

"My name is Mallca," I whispered to myself hoping somehow he heard me and quit calling me that.

Figuring I was not going to get away with not doing it I may as well get this over with. If I was going to fall I might as well get that over with as well. I looked down at my hands wondering how well I was going handle climbing or even get a grip. From the years of carrying supplies back and forth had torn up my hands leaving them with cuts. Luckily they had healed by that time, but gripping was kind of uncomfortable. However, the advantage of the manual labor made my muscles much stronger. If I could bare being uncomfortable for like five minutes then I would be home free.

As I began to climb it seemed like a breeze as I was barely winded. I went up smoothly as everyone watched, but I was exhausted when I reached the top. Does this look fun, amusing to these people? I would have liked to him try this because letting go and falling actually sounded like a good idea.

"Good! That is how to do it! I'm glad someone shows how to get the work done and put in some effort, now climb down!" he called up.

Damn myself and the teacher, who I learned to be Mr. Rogers.

Their goes an idea started as a thought and into an action. During the time I was traveling down I slowly put my foot down and missed the pedal. I fell at the seven foot mark.

I slammed down hard on my back making a sound the people winced at. Well, it was not the first time I had fallen flat on my back that day and I was just getting over the one I had received earlier that morning. Anyone who was in the gym had rushed over to see if I was alright. Having the wind knocked right out of me made it impossible for me to reply. Instead I groaned and tried to get up. Gently Mr. Rogers leaned down to assist me and grabbed my arm. Unfortunatly he grabbed the one with my mark. What I didn't notice was my shirt had come up in two places being my left arm sleeve and my backside. Also some students got touchy to see if I was bruised or anything on the back. Some marks can reveal all secrets or give the people the wrong idea. As everyone saw the whips and the wyvern they gasped knowing all too well what those meant. Usually it gave the wrong idea.

My arm then was forcefully grabbed by Mr. Rogers as he began to drag me into a separate hallway just off the gym.

"If any of you follow you will have dentition for a month!" he shouted right in my ear, but that was not what had set me off. The grip, pull, and reminders came back scaring me.

'No, no, they will not take me back! I didn't do anything!' All the memories are coming back and I had to fight back to protect myself again. If I didn't I would be dead.

Forcefully I pulled back my arm out of his grasp moving away placing distance between us. If he couldn't touch me, he couldn't hurt me both the mental and physical kind. My moments were not quick enough as he grabbed my arm once again and then moving up to my shoulders. He then pinned me against the cold wall sternly trying to find my eyes.

"Have you been there?" he asked assuming I know the 'there' he was referring to. Well, I did.

"Yes." I let a few tears that I was ashamed to release in my crying voice.

"Why?" he asked in a gentler tone, but that did not make any of that better. Mr. Rogers still did what he did and nothing would change that. I then regained myself and was ready to take on anyone, including Batson.

"Because I was not going to be someone who I did not want to be and live by it as some mindless slave that decides just to go with it," I replied in the same manner, confidence in my voice, as went I told Maurus why I took the whip to the face. Sadly that stream of confidence did not last long as I broke again. I could not stand to look at him anymore so I turned away showing the side of my face with the scar. I had been telling people I had hit myself with a sparkler when I was little. Upon seeing it the previously raged yet concerned teacher stepped back allowing me to escape. I did not move an inch. He took this chance to asked questions.

"What happened?" he asked. Most people have the urge to touch it, but he seemed to hold it back.

"I was . . . whipped," I sobbed out, "for protecting . . . my brother . . . who later . . . died." I got out as much I could before I cried so much I could not speak.

Mr. Rogers did not answer me. I was sure he did not know what to say as most people never do. Usually they are all speechless that I have survived something as major as this. The only words he said afterwards were to go get changed and wait for the bell to ring. We had been in the hallway roughly seven minutes and no one dared to pursue. That was the first time I had actually cried about what happened in front of someone I did not know. He was just an ear of a stranger that was willing to listen.

I was wrong when I said no one followed us, some were hiding out in the locker room, and they heard every word. Of course in the high school grape vine it does not take for word to spread. They all knew that I had been to Prison 17-70 and broke my Predetermine. I was the school outcast that only seemed to bring trouble.

I had really hoped having lunch with Atticus, but that was another downfall to today. With the school having about five hundred students caused the school to have two lunch periods and during the other's it was a study hall type of class. After getting what had seemed to look like lunch I sat by myself, isolated, silently eating. No one bother to mess with me or even try to make any connections, which I happen to be grateful for. I was tired and my body ached especially my back.

During lunch, which was some kind of spaghetti, I got a few strange looks from some of the students. A few were moving their head just to get a better look at something. What was it? Did I have something in my teeth or my face? Knowing that it was not my lunch I knew what they were trying to look at; the scar on my face. I knew it was visible, but it wasn't some new fashion sense. At least no one can see the ones on my back, only Atticus has seen those or the wyvern as I wore long sleeves. I was not just tired, depressed, and I kept thinking that it was just going to get worse.

When my lunch ended I saw that Atticus was walking with a group of other students having what seemed to be a nice conversation. He had some kind of a smile on his face and some girl seemed to all over him. Lucky I had to go to class or would have told her a few words on my mind. Sadly I had to pass right by them to go to my study hall and I did not have the most ecstatic face. Atticus saw this and instantly became worried.

"Hey guys I'll meet you up in a minute," he said before coming over to me, "Are you okay?" He could tell that I had been recently crying, a lot.

"I'm fine," I answered trying to hide what he already saw.

"You have been saying that about everything lately," he replied grabbing my hand.

"I have to get to study hall," I said pulling away my hand and walking away.

I knew I left feeling hurt and on a bad note, but it was not the time or place to talk. He should feel privileged that he was the only person in the world I would ever talk to about what happened. A counselor does not know what it feels like and only gives sympathy. I want empathy. Also would they even want to talk to someone like me; I know I wouldn't. Knowing with my problems I'd probably end up giving the counselor a therapist or counseling. I would rather talk at home where I know I have some safety then here with him and five hundred of my closest friends.

Silence became a familiar way to me that day and it so easy to become attached. All the teachers had to introduce me as I would not speak. Everyone did not need to know my name because I was knew by a label that had already been placed, the senior girl who broke her Predetermine and was nothing but trouble. People did respect that I wanted to be left alone.

On the bus we got different glares from this morning from everyone. Apparently the bus driver had learned of my secret, but no one knew that Atticus had been to Prison 17-70 too. That was good; he needed this more than I did. Still, the glares toward me were evil that chased me; trying to chase me out of town. However, Atticus got friendly facials that everyone wanted to be his friend. Neither of us talked on the ride home, but that did not mean when we arrived.

I was relieved when I noticed that we were going to be the first people off the bus. The system was first on, last off, and versa. I made sure I sat near the front so I could be off as soon as possible in order to be faster away from these demons. I walked in the door and almost forgot that Atticus was behind me. Lucky I caught myself before slamming the door in his face, like Vaughan did to me; the feeling which I know all too well. Atticus did not snap as he saw I stopped myself, but he had much more on his mind.

"Mallca, will you please tell me what has been going on?" he asked after getting inside and closing the door.

"No . . ." I mumbled. Yes, yes there was something, but I have no idea where I can possibly start, and how to mold twenty-six letters into perfect sentences to explain to you what's on my mind.

"Please talk to me." I shook my head. "What happened?"

This obviously was not a fight I was going to win if he kept prodding me with questions. He would keep asking if I was alright until I would break. I know that some people, including me, if you ask them if they are alright too many times they will break and tell what is really going on. Obliviously they are not alright and I was just wearing it like a mask hoping to cover up. I guess I had to try and start somewhere.

"You could say that I was attacked today both mentally and physically. The entire school, student and staff, now know who I am and what I have done. That I am married to an unknown guy and that I have broken my Predetermine. My gym teacher dragged me out in the hallway after accidently discovering my marks and questioned me. I felt interrogated," I explained. Atticus was about to speak, but I was not finished yet. "Then I saw you adjusting and fitting in like a new kid. You and those other kid . . . you seem to be moving on while I am haunted by this!"

I never got finish all what I wanted to say and it seemed like I did not want to know what else I could have said. I just stared at him with the tears rushing down from my eyes and dripping off my face. The expression 'cry me a river' was literally what I was doing when it said. Lucky I had not lost my breath yet. I fell to the couch with my head buried into a pillow. I think I may have tried to suffocate myself I was buried so deep. Atticus though of a smart comment about the pillow tasting good to me, but decided this was not the best time. He never did answer me instead he sat on the floor beside me and rubbed my head. I looked up only to find that I was embracing him and sobbing into his chest.

Chapter

11

That night had brought Atticus and me even closer as a couple. I think we have the strongest bond and no one can take that away. They would have to force me to do it because I will not do it willing. One hundred percent, that is how sure I am about that Atticus feels the same. No one dared to try and take him away, now that Atticus had revealed that he was the one I was married to.

To my own surprise going back to school was not as bad as I originally thought. At first people hated me, bumped me into lockers, called me names, fights, and all those immature ways to pick on someone, but after a couple months it all died down and people began to see that I was not as bad. Conversations were started with me and all views on me were eliminated. Some of the people that first started this change were people I use to friends with. I reconnected with them and even made new ones. However, it had to be some curse that I did not have lunch with any of them so I still sat by myself.

They all understood my reasoning for my actions they all came to reason. I had to actually stop a riot before people did what they would have regretted. The students who talked to me were actually going to break their Predetermines to stand up. They said they could not punish them all, but I knew they would find a way. Having them turn on each other to get the traitors. I could not allow that to happen. They would have similar experiences to my own. I even told them what I went through. Lucky enough it opened their minds and got a clue about what I meant. So then I was known as the troubled girl that is kind of cool and I could live with that label.

It had been a peaceful day and I just got my lunch which was a salad that day. I often went between salad and school lunch, just depended on what it was. Anyway, I went to my usual spot to eat alone and even though my standards may have increased, but that did not mean much when you're anti-social. Being alone was something I did not mind after getting used to it for the first two months. It gave me time to think about what I wanted; what was on my mind? In my mind I was always alone with my thoughts, but not on the physical plane.

"Can I help you?" I asked finally noticing that someone was actually sitting in front of me. He was a boy about my age, which was eighteen by then, with dirty blonde hair and green eyes.

"I can't sit with someone who is all by themselves," he answered.

"I am perfectly fine," I pointed out clearly. I made sure I was polite and this was my way of saying leave me alone to be alone.

"I bet you are."

I saw his eyes travel! This guy was checking me out! Did anyone think to talk to him and tell him that I was happily married to Atticus? If only I could slap him on the back of the head without getting in trouble because I would do it. Knowing if Atticus everfound out he would smack this kid too, ooh, double team. Without him seeing me I rolled my eyes at the fact he was flirting on me.

"Oh please . . ." I mumbled, "I have a boyfriend." So I'm married, is it not the same thing in reality? We are still together, just bound by matrimony.

"I know, I heard from some other people," he said. I guess he knew when I said boyfriend, I meant husband. "I'm Severn."

"Mallca," I answered. I was taught never to be rude and not answer someone when they were talking to me, especially when introducing themselves.

"That's a nice name for someone like you," he replied.

What did he mean by that? If that was another pick up line, it was not working. See this was why I turned down every guy that ever tried this with me; this was not the way to get a date with me.

Also, about the comment, for his sake, it should have been a good meaning and not insulting. I do not even know what it means. My mother heard it somewhere and knew that her daughter, if she was to have one, should be named that. I do not even know what it means and trust me, I have tried to look it up.

"Thanks . . ." I said politely, but uncomfortable. I really did not want to carry on with this conversation and lucky for me I didn't have too. Before the conversation could go any further or weirder I was literally saved by the bell.

"See you later Mallca," he said getting up from the table.

"Maybe . . ." I said making sure I went in an opposite direction as Severn. I only said something not to leave him hanging, that would be rude, but I couldn't say yes or sure. For all I know he could have just wanted to be friends and I seemed like a nice person. However, the way I was reading this guy he looked like he wanted to be the guy friend more than my friend and that actually happened to me; Atticus was my best friend and later became my husband.

Speaking of Atticus, I did not tell him about Severn and it was best to keep it that way. I was not protecting him, I was just keeping Atticus from freaking out or seeing this guy as a threat to our relationship. If he thought that he was, he probably would go up to him and give a warning to step away from me. True, that would be sweet and all, but he does not need to scare the guy. Plus, he really did not do anything except flirt with me and what guy hasn't done that. With Atticus, all the guy had to do is whistle or touch for him to snap unless I did first. It makes them think twice about me. Atticus does not seem like the protective boyfriend type, but he is, even if he does not like to show it.

With most guys the flirting is usually stopped after the first try, unless they mentally do not understand that I am not interested in them and that has happened before. After I decline the offer we usually try to return to our previous standards with each other. With my crushes, they stay as a secret to only me, or between my female friends. It would have been weird to discuss that subject that this guy is cute with Atticus. Plus, I did not have the guts to ask them out. Just the feeling of rejection just scares me and I know I should have gotten out there, but it is too late for that. Sadly I was wrong when I saw him sitting where he was yesterday, across from me, the next day at lunch. I looked to find another place to sit, but that would be rude. Nope, that was not the reason; I couldn't find another place to sit. So I didn't have a choice not to go there and there would be unwanted conversation.

"Can I help you with something? Did I do something that makes you think about me being a friend or something? I just don't understand," I asked placing my tray on the table.

"No, I'm new here and I heard that you are too. Plus, you look lonely here and I thought you would want some company," he explained.

"I arrived here months ago," I informed him.

"Just sit down, it is not going to hurt you," he said placing his hand upon mine. Quickly I pulled my hand away and reluctantly sat down. Like I had said, I really did not have anywhere else to sit.

I should have made him leave as it was my spot first.

Severn actually kept quiet the entire period and only glanced at me five times. The five times that I saw. These glances were more like stares that lasted about three minutes and were straight into my face.

When people do that I get uncomfortable and want to know what he is staring at. Asking him, 'what the hell was he looking at?' would extremely rude on my part as he was just trying to be nice. Finally this awkward moment finally ended as well as the period. What I also did not know was something I cared for could soon end. Apparently I did not remove my hand fast enough to escape a pair of gossip eyes.

When I say that Atticus was good looking and some girls wished they were me just to be with him I was not kidding. Being strong, smart, and caring he almost seemed perfect. Even at the school where we have not been very long was enough for Atticus to attract not only attention, but attraction. Some of those girls would try anything.

"Hey Atticus!" a girl we had known to be named Merrilla said walking up to him and interlocking her arm with him. Merrilla was the girl that wants to be both your friend and your girlfriend that no one can ditch.

"Hi?" he questioned her being so touchy. It would take an idiot not to notice that she was flirting with him.

"I think I saw something today that you might be interested in," she said getting in front of him so he would look at her when she was talking to him. She was also petting his shoulder with her index finger. She was damn lucky I wasn't around or she would have never pointed with that finger again. Atticus was not the only protective one; I had him and I wasn't going to let him go.

"I bet you did and that I would love to know," Atticus said. He hanged around me too much; he had picked up my sarcasm. He also had hoped she would say "I see how happy you are with Mallca and decided to leave you two alone." Unfortunately those were not even close to what she was about to tell him.

"I saw Mallca with Severn today with his hand on top of hers and she didn't move. She looked comfortable with his hand on hers. I think there is something going on between them. You know what I mean?"

Atticus knew exactly what she meant and it made him furious. There was a possibility that I was cheating on him with some new guy that I had barely knew. Atticus is the one that tends to overreact and not stop to think that it could be all a mistake. Also his source was not reliable one. He felt betrayed. I had no knowledge that Merrilla had seen what had happened at lunch that day or that she had told Atticus. On the bus ride home he did not speak to me when I tried or even sit with me when I made room. He had this perturbed looked and was about ready to snap on the untended target. I thought he had a bad day and just did not want anyone right now. That was something I could understand. I figured I would try his approach to me that one day and try speaking to him on the walk up to home, also an unsuccessful attempt. As we got where we were in opposite positions as before when I was upset. Atticus was in the front and I was following behind. Except I had caught myself not shutting the door in his face while he slammed it violently shut. Lucky I stepped back in time just to avoid injury. He made me furious and confused which is never a good mixture. I was going to make him talk to me if he wanted to or not. I composed myself not to sound angry, but that was unsuccessful.

"What was that for?" I snapped coming in shutting the door behind me in a similar matter as he just did.

"You know what it was for!" he replied diving onto the couch. I was really confused and it clearly showed on my face. Also getting him to talk to me was easier than I thought it was going to be.

"I actually don't know so you mind giving me a couple hints," I stated.

"Don't play dumb with me! That is just going to make you even guiltier and I won't be surprised if they don't take you away again for being a breaker!"

This was getting worse by the second and his choice of words did not make the situation any better.

"First of all, I am not playing dumb! And second, I have not broken anything and I have been playing my cards right! I have no idea what you are talking about!"

Atticus figured I was not going to confess unless he knew actually what I was doing; it was easier just point it out.

"Merrilla saw you and Severn hand in hand today! You're cheating on me!" he shouted getting up.

"And you believe her! Atticus that's low . . . even for you." I said in a softer upset tone. It was official we had our first fight as a married couple.

"What does that mean?" he asked sensing my mood had calmed.

"Never mind, you're dense," I muttered before going toward the door. I couldn't take his stubbornness any longer and it was always been best for me to walk away before making the problem any worse.

"Mallca wait!" he cried, but I was already out the door.

At first I did not know where I could go to escape this madness and I also knew Atticus would be behind in no time at all. So I had to think fast. My house was not an option as other people lived inside its walls. Going back inside would just mean facing the problem sooner than I wanted too. Finally my mind decided on the perfect place. I had not been there in a while and it had this calming effect except when Bethany decided to try it too after we had specifically told her not too. It was time I regain my ability to be a bird, I guess now wyvern, and fly up and away into hiding.

As I left to my spot Atticus had just came outside. He figured I was just sitting on the porch balling my eyes out about what had just occurred, but he should know me better than that. Lucky for him it was still bright out, so spotting me would not be as hard as at night. Also in the game of hide and seek I was never very good because I always made noise.

Orange, brown, even green leaves crunched beneath my feet as I ran through the back yard toward my destination. When I got to the tree it had grown bigger since the last time I saw it, but not by much. It still kept the path I used to get to the top. When I climbed it did seem like I would just either fly or levitate to the comfortable spot that I could lay on the branch. I could see all on the ground and no one could see me as I was camouflaged by the thick shrubs of leaves. Before this all happened we would play laser tag and this would be my sniper position; I wish I had that gun and could push back any invaders.

Atticus had followed the crunching sound and path to the backyard to find the trail had gone cold. That was an obvious sign that I was in the area, ready to strike, but not this time. I was using this to hide. I slowed my hard breathing to small and silent. Even in the day I could be a black cat hiding in the night's shadows.

"Mallca I know you're out here!" he called and he was right. Of course I didn't answer.

Atticus then realized where he was at in the yard. He found himself looking at the tree we had climbed as children and where Bethany fell. He smiled and shook his head knowing my location and started toward the tree. "Fine then, I guess I will have to come and get you myself."

"No!" I yelled. I only said something to keep him on the ground for I did not want to see his face and I was not sure the branches could hold us both.

"Fine, I'll start. What did you mean by what you said before you left?" he asked.

"Merrilla has been after you since we arrived and learned that you had a girlfriend, which happens to be your wife. You should know she's a flirt that will try anything to take you away from me. I think Severn is trying to do the same with me. You and I seem to have faith bringing us together by the Predetermine and it is theirs to break us apart," I explained. I never thought I could say such somewhat heart-felt words.

"What are you trying to say?" he asked. He was pushing for a couple words I never liked to say, but he waited just minutes longer because I was climbing down when a branch broke. I fell not a long distance and was able to catch myself. Leaves fell with me and were tangled in my hair.

"Mallca!" Atticus said seeing me hit the ground safely on both feet. "Are you okay?" he actually started to laugh at me by my appearance and the fact that I fell out.

"I'm fine," I replied beginning to laugh myself.

"Now what were you trying to say?" he asked.

"I was trying to say that I lo . . . lov . . ." I stuttered. He then kissed me and I was able to say, "I love you."

His face had calmed down from the last time I saw it and I hoping not to get all teary eyed. I can be deeply emotional when the time is right. I had to tell him I was never going to leave him hopefully anytime soon.

"I'm sorry about what I said to you. I didn't mean any of it," he apologized.

"I know. You were upset and as confused as I was," I replied hugging him providing comfort for the both of us.

"So do you think it is in their Predetermine to break us apart?" he asked breaking the hug off and staring at me.

"You know that I don't think about this kind of stuff; it is implied that I know," I answered bring his a smile to his face. That was what I wanted to see and it made me smile too.

"Do you think we should question them about it?" he asked.

"What did I just tell you about me thinking?" I asked playing around.

"It is implied that you know," he replied smirking.

"Other than that I think that it is a good idea."

The next day at school our plan went into action to stop this mess with our love life. We each met with our according people and asked them to meet us after school outside the front door when everyone had cleared out for the day. Hearing that we wanted to meet them made them think that they were successful. They did not know how wrong they were because they had brought us closer.

"Hey Merrilla," said Severn seeing her walking toward him.

"Hi, have you seen Atticus? He told me to meet him here today after school?" she answered.

"Mallca told me the same during lunch," he replied.

"We need to talk to you two," I said coming out the door.

"About us?" he said getting all seductive with me and having the wrong idea.

"Then why am I here?" Merrilla asked. I just wanted to tell her to shut up, but that would ruin the idea.

"If you hold on she would get to that and Mallca was talking about us," Atticus said coming out the same door I did and took my hand.

Severn was speechless when my protective husband came out taking me by the hand with his fingers intertwined with mine. Merrilla looked like Atticus had betrayed her, but he was never hers in the first place. With our hands locked it kept us from popping the other's secret lover in the jaw, but it was not really a secret.

"Why?" I asked. Severn looked like he was playing dumb, but Atticus got this last night. The acting of I don't know what you are talking about deal, but I was not acting. He knows it works to get to what they did to make them talk and not play their games.

"Why were you coming after us?" Atticus snapped.

"We don't have a choice or we would become just like you two,"

Severn explained for them both as Merrilla did not want to talk about it. Despite, the way she acts, she's actually kind of shy.

At first I did not understand what he was talking about by, like us, but then I saw him gesturing toward my arm, the wyvern.

They did not have marks like we had, but if not completing their Predetermine they would. It was what I thought about the night before, it being their Predetermine.

"It is your Predetermine . . ." I whispered. They each had nodded slightly confirming my suspicions.

"The romantic part at least is to steal away another's that are happy as you are. Severn is the same way. After we found out about each other's, we said we would work together in finding the couple.

It would make it easier on us both. Then we saw you two after Atticus revealed that you were his girlfriend and knew that you could be the ones," Merrilla explained.

The Predetermine was getting sicker as I found out more about it and what it was doing to people. I guess that if people won't break their Predetermine I guess they will see to that the bearers cannot complete it. Four people in our area caused each one of us either great pain or rare sight of happiness. Making innocent people do what they are told to do or they have the chance of dying. I saw what their motto is . . . life is what they make it and you will follow it. I was more compelled to end this. As much as I don't really like them, I can't help to want to save them.

Before I could actually end the Predetermine I had to finish my senior year of high school. Everyone said that it would go by so fast, but that was a matter of opinion. I had forgotten who had told me this, but they were right. They said, "The weekend goes by in like in minutes, but why does it take like forever for one class period." However, one of my classes could last forever as this one seemed twenty minutes. It was my AP (Advanced Placement) English Class and that was one of three classes I had with Atticus.

I walked in to see everyone waiting for class to get started and eventually end. Atticus and I agreed that we would keep our distance from each other for safety. I almost fought with him about this, because I wanted to be near him. The people around me improved on their behavior especially when I made it clear until I was out of high school I was to go by Siyas, not Siyas-Issigna. The bell rang and the teacher came asking us all to quiet down, oddly we were already quiet.

That day was discussion day, but what day wasn't. We all sat in different shapes so we all could look at one another in not such a classroom type fashion and still talk to each other. Atticus sat across from me and a few times I caught him staring at me. From there he would go straight into a smile. I could not help but smile in return.

When no one noticed I would just look at Atticus or I was smart and took the chance whenever he putting forth his input. He was (and still is) my cute and intelligent guy and no one else's. I have already had this proven fact with Merrilla and if anyone wasn't too smart to notice they would learn what she did. I remembered what times use to be like in school. When I looked at him all I see my husband and my best friend, then, he was my partner in crime. We'd cause trouble without making a huge dilemma. I wished we could go back before this all started, like having a life's undo button. I also wished I had paid attention to our discussions.

"Mallca, what do you get from the story?" the teacher asked. I read the book so I knew what going on and thankfully the question was asking me of my own opinion so there really isn't a wrong answer.

"I believe that love is the strongest and life should be what you decide, because I remember hearing that it is never too late," I answered. Everyone in the class just stared at me speechless, because that's what I think. The teacher told me two things, that was what she wanted to hear, and that what she thinks too. All I could was smile. People were on my side.

School ended in no time after that and it was time for graduation that May. I remember that I did not want to go for the fact that there would be people there. No one would be there to cheer for me or Atticus, so what was the point of going. Also I had nothing to wear anyway. All my clothes I had before were lost when my house was taken over. Since we have returned I either got them free or I borrowed from Daphnia's closet. I never liked to do so, but I could not wear the same mangled clothes every day and Atticus said it was okay. He told me to search for one of her dresses she had worn when she was my age and planned on giving to Bethany; I found the dress. It was blue with a black covering and the dress itself was strapless. The covering acted as sleeves holding it up. It was beautiful and I loved it. However, I was hesitant in wearing it because it was not mine to take. Atticus said it was okay and that his family would want me to have it. The dress was a perfect fit like it was made for me.

Graduation was held outside on the football field with the guest in the stands waiting for their child or even children to cross. These were all unfamiliar faces to me and Atticus. Some I have seen before, but it was likely that they would remember me. It was hot outside and the purple robes did not make it any better. We sat listening to each speaker go up and make their speech. I kept thinking none of this applied to me as the principal said he knew these kids for four years. Atticus and I were not sitting together because of my choice to keep my last name, Issigna and Siyas. However, I could see him where I was sitting. I looked down at the metal nut on my finger and thought that this wasn't real.

"May the next row stand," the principal said. That was Atticus's row. I heard other names before his.

"Atticus Joseph Issigna," he said. I cheered for him and he heard me. I figured that someone should at least cheer for him. It looked like I had embarrassed him, but I didn't care. It is also my job to embarrass him. It said that I loved him. About two more rows went by before mine.

"Mallca Azria Siyas," the next announcer said being the vice principal. I walked toward the stand and took my diploma, shaking each of the hands of the education providers. People clapped for the fact, but no cheers. Then I heard the loudest cheer coming from behind me. It was Atticus and it was my turn to be embarrassed. As I walked by him I mouth that I loved him. He said it back, but he looked more emotional with it than I did. I wonder why and I found out when I got home.

Before we walked in Atticus grabbed me by the hand and turned me around. He was on the wooden floor of the porch down on one knee and taking out a box. I knew what it was from the moment I saw it. He slipped off the metal nut and opened the box. He took out a shiny ring with a diamond and smaller ones embedded around it the ring was beautiful too. Like with the dress, I was speechless.

"I never got to actually do this to you in real life so now I have the chance when you look so beautiful now. Not that you don't you look beautiful every day," he said. I smiled and shook my head at his suck-up comment. He always knows how to make me smile.

"I figured that if you are my wife you would need a real ring. I have one too; they belonged to my mom and dad. In her will she told me that these were for you and me."

"I . . . can't . . . take this," I stuttered out.

"Yes you can, because it is supposed to be this way."

Without any more words he kissed me as he had always done before. When he released my lips I automatically went back as I didn't want that time between us to end. We knew each other was for the other one. The right man for me was right in front of me and he was my best friend. I knew I had even more to fight for for freedom.

Chapter

12

Breathing heavily from exhaustion and the unbearable pain was all familiar to my body. Where was I at? I cannot see what is around me because it all dark and cloudy. There is a building and the people are all shadows. Then the shadow figures become clearer and I knew where I was at. The rough terrain I walk on bare foot and the logs in my hand that scratch up both my hands and arms are much worse than the first time. I can no longer recognize them or hold the logs that I carry on an endless route. To feel relief I drop the logs and as soon as they hit the ground he appeared. It may have looked weak, but as he appeared I fell along with the logs. The man standing before me looking down at my broken and hurting body was Batson. For dropping the logs I take ten whips. He already has it in his hands and was ready for me to make a mistake. I scream as each one slaps across my back and each sound gets louder as it continues. After the tenth I expect this all to stop and disappear, but it doesn't end. Eleven, twelve, thirteen, and the whips just keep going. I no longer felt the pain and nothing more. I have returned to this hell again and I couldn't escape.

I heard a faint voice in the crowd scream at me to be strong and fight it. It sounded distorted and I can't make it out. It said not to give into Batson because that's what he wants. The voice is being dragged away and I can no longer hear it. I'm left with the man known as the devil here. The crowd only stares at me doing nothing out what can be either fear or the love of watching. I couldn't tell who the voice was, but at least someone guided me out, even if it was for a little while. Finally it stopped at . . . I had lost count, but it was about sixty. I was on my knees the entire time and as soon as my destroyed body is able to fall . . . it does.

As I hit the ground a dust cloud was made and I jumped up wide eyed from my bed. My skin and clothes are drenched with my cold sweat. My lungs were working overtime to catch my breath which was rapid like I had just run a marathon.

Caught up to my surroundings I found myself back in my bedroom, at the moment the safest place I could have been. Atticus was deeply sleeping beside me not knowing I had just woken up from a horrid nightmare. I was tired, but I couldn't go back to sleep, not like this. I wouldn't go back. I found myself back at Prison 17-70. Face to face with my worst enemy and fear. Cautiously I laid back down staring out the window waiting for the sun to rise.

While lying there I allowed my mind just wonder from sorts of different ideas from my dreams to the fact that my feet are freezing even though I wore socks to bed. When the clock struck seven in the morning I decided that I should get up and start my morning routine. Maybe going through it would help clear my jumbled and frighten mind. I walked slowly into the bathroom, turned on the light, looking into the mirror at the dark circles around my eyes. That was not the first night and it would not be my last. The nightmares started a month after getting back to civilization and the one I had that night was the worst. It seemed like that was the only way they were getting. Yes, I had barely slept. My stubbornness and fears kept these secrets hidden and that was the way I had wanted to keep it.

My daily routine was pretty much average, like any person in the world. I get up and begin with taking a shower. I snuck over to my drawer and pulled out some clothes and undergarments for today and returned to the bathroom. I tried not to wake Atticus and that wasn't difficult to accomplish as the guy can sleep through a hurricane. More like tornado from the story I heard before meeting him.

After I turned on the light I shut my eyes to shield them from at the moment bright lights. It was like I had walked outside after coming out from a dark cave. I guess I have to wait for my eyes to adjust. Slowly I undressed down to my undergarments and turned on the warm to hot water. I looked in the mirror seeing my scars, but I don't allow them to bother me. After removing the rest of my clothes I hopped in the shower hoping to wash it all away, but I only felt the water run down my body. When I was done I should have gone back to bed, but that would have never happened.

After I had gotten dressed I went down stairs to sit on the couch all alone in the dark. It was as peaceful here as it usually was and it was a good place to think. I thought about my dreams and all that had gone on in the last five years. I was surprised I hadn't cried or broke down and committed suicide yet. Only minutes went by before I decided to end this sadness and I opened a curtain to allow light to brighten up the room. I thought about breakfast quickly turning it down noticing within myself I did not have the ability to eat. I returned to sitting on the couch silently thinking about my previous thoughts. I was so deep in thought that I did not hear Atticus come down.

"I didn't hear you get up," he said coming off the steps.

"I haven't been up very long," I lied. Looking at the clock I see that it is already nine meaning I have been up for four hours already. I never even noticed how fast really went by.

"I doubt that."

"Whatever," I said smirking before going back upstairs.

Going into the sun filled bedroom I forgot what I had originally went up there to do, or did I even have a reason in the first place? I just decided to sit down on the bed and just doing that made me drowsy. My eyes kept falling and my body swayed. Even awake the memories returned in my daydreams, more like a nightmare in the day.

I heard the screams from the night we all tried for a prison break. I heard everything, not just only seeing the images, but the screams and surrounding gunfire. My ears hurt with the loud cracks one after another with the death that shortly followed. My body is like a ghost that can only watch as this all plays out like a movie. As the prisoners attempt to run away they fall down as a bullet pierce their bodies through the back or trip either on their own feet or the dead companions. My eyes wander around the area and I see a horrid sight. It is my little brother Vaughan lying on the ground. He looks cold to the touch and his eyes are wide open. It seems like some hit him with a car because his position on the ground and his eyes look like he could have been. I tried to run and kneel down to him hoping that this was all some sick joke he decided to play on me, but I was unable to move. My feet felt as if they have been anchored to the ground set never to move. I then tried to call out, but I had no voice. I only seemed like a body of nothing that could only stand and watch as her brother died in front of her.

I was enclosed so deeply in my nightmare that I never heard Atticus enter the bedroom and walk over toward me. It wasn't until he touched me that I knew he was there. I jumped up what seemed like a foot off the bed. I probably did because of the springs. When I looked at him he had this apologetic face.

"I thought you heard me come in," he snickered. He thought it was funny I didn't.

"No, I didn't," I answered masking my fear with smile and a playful tone.

"Ready?" he asked.

"Get ready for what?" I exclaimed. I had no idea what he was talking about or I just forgot, most likely the second one in my case.

"We have that welcoming party to our neighbors just down the road," he explained.

"I don't want to go." My tone had just made a one-eighty. I had my reasons not to go; I was tired and the fact that the house we were going to was mine or use to be.

"Please. You need to get past this and this is a way that you can do it," he told me like he was my shrink and that was someone I don't want. If I had to it would be called me, myself, and I. Seriously, he's like my best friend, my therapist, my husband, but I love him anyway. However, like those nut cases, they are usually right. I don't know how, but agreed to return to that house.

It now belonged to a family of four, just like the Siyas family was before the Predetermine. I actually think the house attracts people that have a last name starting with "S" because they are the Scarlings. He was to a businessman while she was to be a house wife and take care of their kids.

"Hello! Oh, I'm so glad you could make it," Mrs. Scarlings said as she opened door.

"It was not a problem, we're glad you invited us," Atticus replied being the most polite of the two of us and I was probably going to say something I'd regret.

"Hello, I'm Mr. Scarlings, but you can call me Sergio," said the owner.

"Hi, I'm Atticus Issigna and this is my wife Mallca."

The two men, even though they were about ten years apart seemed to talking well. I just wanted to bolt for home, but if Atticus was having a good time, why should I ruin it for him? I just stood there and listen to their conversation. A couple times I was tempted to fine Rachel Scarlings, the wife, and see if I could start talking with her, but that woman was a social butterfly and her husband agreed.

"I looked up this house and I saw the most intriguing feature about it. Every member of the previous family in this house had broken their Predetermine and they all died. I tell my kids not tobe like them as they are examples of what happens when the law is broken," he mentioned.

"You don't know what you're talking about . . ." I mumbled.

"Excuse me?" Sergio asked.

"I'm still alive. Do you know the last name of the people who use to live here?" I asked rather coldly.

"Yes, it was like Siyas or something."

"Yeah, I may be married to Atticus, but my last name is Siyas. That's right I'm the eldest daughter of the Siyas family."

"I'm sorry. I didn't know," he apologized. I could tell he was meaning it, but I was just to upset.

"No, of course not, because I'm dead," I answered taking his own words or so called facts. I just decided it was best for me to leave and not get any more involved, if he wishes too, then he can come to my territory. As I was making my way to the door a Dalmatian dog, I learned her name to be Dotty later, was also at the door wanting outside. She looked at me as if I was going to take her outside for a walk.

"Sorry. She's friendly with anyone and probably thinks that you are going to take her out. Honey, could you throw me her leash," Rachel said. She had missed the conversation seconds ago so to her I was an innocent neighbor.

Sergio complied with her demand grabbing a black leash of the hook on the wall and began tossing it to her. I turned to see his reaction toward me seeing the leash had come undone and was coming at me. I turned and ended up getting smacked on the side of the head with the hook metal part. Then everything in my scenery changed. Sergio looked like Batson, Atticus who rushed to me looked like Maurus, and Rachel on my right was Romone.

Worst of all, the leash was the whip.

"Mallca!" Atticus said.

I had dropped to my knees and began to cry. The smack didn't hurt, but it was what it brought forth that caused me pain, all the dreaded memories. The memories I was hoping to leave behind.

"Is she okay?" Sergio asked.

"I don't know. She had a bad experience . . . I think we'll just leave. We're causing a problem from being here, sorry for the problem," Atticus apologized taking me by the wrist and shoulders guiding me out.

The way it felt he had a hold of me was like I was being dragged out for another whipping. Of course I struggled to get away. I would not go through another one of those because once was enough. Atticus tried to calm me down with words, but nothing helped. I finally broke free and rushed inside the house straight up the stairs to our room. I slammed the door and dove on the bed giving me some comfort. I heard the creaking steps and the door opened. It was Atticus, but it wasn't, it was Batson.

"Stay Away!" I screamed moving to the dark corner. I had to escape the reaper of my nightmares.

"Mallca . . ." Atticus said softly not to provoke me. My mind was so messed up and dizzy. It was like having a headache and reading something then someone takes it away extremely fast. The room was basically spinning. Neither of us understood what was going on.

It was obvious that I was in a dangerous emotional state so messing with me would not be the best move right now.

"Mallca?" he called again. The room was a deep, dark black, he couldn't see me.

"Go away . . ." I muttered.

"I'm sorry, but I won't do that to you." Atticus said. Knowing him, he would be the one to tell me that, but the moment I'll believe anything, even if it is the truth or a lie.

"Yes you will . . ."

I have never been more bewildered in my life. Everything that surrounded me was such a major blur and so was that moment.

Like it was another person living this moment and I am a spectator in all this. Atticus's eyes finally adjusted to the darkness and he located me in the corner of the room with my knees held close to my chest. I heard him step closer to me. Escape was not one of my options at that moment. He hovered over me for a few moments before he leaned against the wall and slid down to sit beside me. I knew he would place his arms around me and I just leaned in to meet him. His strong chest was so comfortable and I felt safe. It was safer than I had felt in long time.

"Want to tell me about what happened when you were leaving?" he softly asked as he moved my hair from my face.

I shakily answered, "It felt like I was back at that day when the leash crossed my face. You know, with Batson, when everything just started to all go wrong. It seems like everything is that way now. Someone has taken my memories and placed them outside into the real world of my life."

As I finished talking I began to cry and caressed my hair to silence me. Before I realized I had fallen asleep there in the corner on Atticus's shoulder. I think after five minutes of watching me sleep he decided that he should too. That night I didn't have dreams about the days I had been inside the prison, but the final day, the day I was released.

It seemed only as I was just reliving the moment. Was that a way for my subconscious mind to release me from my agonizing nightmares? I heard all the symbols being called out and everyone stepping up. Most people would believe these people are more likely to die than be released. Neither of us has been called up, never mind, Atticus was just called. Just as it happened he cautiously walked up after kissing me and the suspense started. At least I knew that I would be out of here soon and I would get to see, in my opinion, the hilarious face on Batson as he called out the wyvern. The entire time when it actually happened Atticus stayed eye locked with me, but he won't even glance at me. More marks are called, but mine isn't and Atticus isn't looking at me. What's going on? Finally the releasing has ended and I am among the people that are still left here to suffer. My worst fear that day has come alive. Atticus doesn't look shocked or that he cares. I run up to him and he just pushes me away telling me he only married me so he could stay alive. He is entirely different man than the person who kissed me moments ago. I am now all alone and even Maurus will not acknowledge me especially when I am in need of his help. He claims he only helped me because he didn't know what kind of terrible person I was until now. I don't get released until a year later, but the damage is already done. My mind is gone and my physical body is weary as in any moment I could collapse. Batson and his men worked me harder than anyone else in the prison. Even if I had not done anything I was the one to blame. As I head toward the exit Batson took one last swig with the whip at me. It smacks me straight in the middle of my back and I jump. I also scream as I fall toward the earth. Again like last night as I hit the ground, I jump up in bed.

"Mallca, it is okay, your fine!" Atticus cooed me holding close so I didn't thrash around and hurt myself or him. He also had a wash cloth and wiped the cold sweat from my forehead. When he held me I could hear his breathing so it allowed me to slow my own.

"It was another nightmare . . ." I answered.

"I know, but I am going to help end those." he said, "Do you want to talk about it?"

I almost wanted to answer him no, but I noticed he would make me sooner or later. To calm my fears of his ulterior motive I had to ask "Do you care about me?"

He wasn't sure what to say. He just began to snort and ask, "Why would you ask such a silly question? Of course I care about you."

". . . even if I didn't come out with you at the first release?"

"Mallca, you don't need to worry about my feeling toward you, those will never change. Mallca, I love you."

That was I all needed to hear from him and as soon I realized what he had said I hugged him. I explained every nightmare that I had since I was released. From my brother, the whippings, to the one I had just had where he no longer loved me and left me to die. Atticus told me these are only nightmares and reassured that they would stay that way. Also, he reminded me dreams are events that already happened so there is no way they could occur again. He gave a similar explanation for my nightmares as they were just reliving the event in a horrid light. I dared them to come back. With my new found confidence I could handle anything.

Chapter

13

Just because my nightmares were over didn't mean that my dreams were to be over. That next night I had another dream, but this one I actually liked. I was content with any dream as long as it didn't remind me of Prison 17-70 and I wouldn't wake up screaming in the middle of the night. This dream only screamed innocent and peaceful.

I found myself standing on the porch of Atticus's house; I guess you say our house too, but that debate is for later. I was in dark jeans and grey shirt with black sleeves. I seemed to out there waiting for something. By my appearance I was not eighteen, but at least twenty-three. I did not look bad for my new age. My hair was longer, but I still had the style I left Prison 17-70 with, actually, the one it had given me. In other ways I still seemed the same. I was an observer on the side standing in the yard. Looking at myself I heard a sound come from the end of street. We both turned our heads to look down to see a school bus heading this way.

Why would I be waiting for a long, yellow school bus? I don't go to school anymore, may be college, but why would I need to take school bus to go there? Unless they found some bizarre way to send me back. I really hoped that wasn't the case. It had been hard enough to handle the first time. I found it a good idea to keep my thoughts quiet and just watch.

The double window doors open and a little girl about seven gets off. She has brown hair and it is up in a ponytail. She has on white sandals and a pink dress. Upon seeing the older version of me she runs up the walkway and hugs me. The girl has the biggest smile plastered on her face; it seems like nothing could take away her happiness and all the madness has been destroyed.

"How was your day?" I asked.

"Good," she answered, "Can I go get a snack then do my homework?"

"Yes."

This could not be my child and I know I am for sure. One reason is my Predetermine says so also I don't want them. Plus, she is too old to be mine and even if she was . . . she definitely takes after Atticus. She wanted to start her homework? It took me hours before I actually wanted to do it and sometimes I didn't even start it. The little girl then ran inside and a man I presumed to be Atticus stepped out. He hadn't change much either, except getting older. He wrapped his arms around me and placed his chin in the crook of my neck. He also placed his hands intertwined on my stomach. He basically wrapped me up in a hug and as I looked upon the two love birds I could almost feel my Atticus doing the exact motion to me.

"She is so much like her mother," he said.

"Yeah, she is. I still miss them, but at least I can say this is all over," I answered.

"True. Your parents would be so proud of you and be thankful for the great job you have done with her."

"Thanks."

Suddenly I heard a break from within the house. I see the older one's head roll back and look inside toward the house.

"Alaina, what happened?"

"What? Nothing happened, it was an accident," I heard.

I could not believe what I was hearing or seeing right then and I am one of those people where I have to see it to believe it. That little girl that I just saw is my little sister, Alaina. She has grown up and is now living with Atticus and me. How was that even possible? Illingsworth took her away from me. How did I even get her back? Before I had anymore thoughts I had opened my eyes to a loud scream.

When I looked to discover the scream I found the noise only to be my alarm clock. I reached over and pushed the snooze button. I wanted to go back to sleep, but I figured my best choice was just to turn my clock off. My clock told me it was eight o'clock so I guessed it was time to get up. It seemed too early, but for me that is any time before eleven. Right then it did not matter because all I thought about was my dream. It did not matter about the time the dream would still just ventured into head. Alaina was safe and where she should be.

The ways that seemed obvious to getting my sister back were the ones that would not work. If I had gone to court about my rights as her blood relative, it would have been dumb idea because Illingsworth controls their system. Only one idea came to mind and it seemed out of the question. Stealing her back had come to my mind? There are only two problems with this idea, the fact I do not know where she is and if I am caught I would be either sent to who knows where or Prison 17-70. Not knowing the poor girl's location canceled the plan of going to Illingsworth and asking him nicely for my sister back. I was thinking of anything I could until Atticus stopped me.

"Hey, I'm going to run a few errands, do you want to come?" he asked me.

"Sure, I'll go with you," I answered getting up and grabbing a sweater off the hanger in the closet.

"Uh, Mallca?" he asked. I just lifted my eyebrows to acknowledge I knew he was attempting to talk to me. "Are you going out like that?"

'Did I look bad?' I thought. All I had on jeans, boots, a long sleeve shirt, and the sweater.

"Sorry, let's go." He was smart to end the conversation right there as I becoming both confused and upset.

I only agreed to run these errands with him to get Alaina off my mind because if I didn't I swore I was going to go crazy just sitting around here thinking about it. Even if it was for a short amount of time it could do me some good. Atticus never told me what his errands were and I wish he had told me sooner as even as an adult I still don't enjoy going to the market.

Atticus and shopping takes the time it takes for some senior citizen or my great grandmother to search down every aisle. Usually it ends in being a waste of time and only end up getting what was intended to get. I could not help to think about when we are that old. I snicker and shutter at the thought meaning that it would take twice as long to accomplish this task. My father told me when I talked about my great grandmother that it was the odd things people do that actually end up helping them later. Never did I once believe him until that day.

Going through what I remember being aisle number thirteen or fourteen, I had lost count and didn't bother to look, I saw a man who was very familiar to me. Atticus would not have recognized him, but why would he? The only people that could recognize him besides me are dead. They were the people who were with me during my Predetermine. The man I saw was Illingsworth.

Why would he be here? Doesn't he have maids or butlers for this kind of stuff? I was confused, unless I was mistaken and this man just happens to look like him. I was almost convinced of this until I saw someone with him that made me turn the opposite direction.

A little girl about the age of four or five who strangely reminded me of the people that were or used to be in my life. They were my entire family, my mother, father, me, and younger brother. Not only them, but the Alaina I had seen in my dream the night before. In my mind I imagined the Alaina I saw down a few ages and it was striking in resemblance to her. I just had to know if this was my little sister.

From what I remembered about Alaina with the time I spent with her was she had a birthmark on her neck that looked like a bruise or a scuff of dirt. Basically someone had darkish tan permanent paint on their thumb and pressed it into her neck. As we walked closer toward the two I looked down to my feet to see my shoe was untied. What luck, I had thought, but actually it was not as lucky as I first intended. When I looked I lost my footing and fallen onto my face. I could hear Atticus just think, *'nice move grace.'* Then again maybe it was luck that I had fallen because I had landed in front of the pair I wanted the closer look at.

"You okay?" the girl asked. She was at perfect eye level with me so it would not look suspicious when I glanced at her neck. I saw what I was looking for; the birthmark was exactly where I had remembered it to be located.

"Yes and thank you for asking," I replied. I wondered if something had gone wrong because the girl just kept staring intently at my face. I thought I had a nasty zit or a mark on my face. Before I could think or say anything the girl raised her hand pointing out with her index finger. The little finger traveled to the side of my face where... yes, I did have mark. She traced down the side as it were a pencil and a line drawn. I knew this was my sister because every time Alaina saw it she was compelled to do the exact same gesture.

"Mallca?" she whispered where only I could hear her. "Yes . . . Alaina?"

Alaina nodded and a slight smile appeared across her face. I felt like grabbing her and running away as far as possible. I was too late because Illingsworth grabbed her hand.

"Sorry," he apologized, "you should know better than to touch people like that."

"No, it is fine," I replied.

Again I was helpless as I watched him do it again; Illingsworth was walking away with my baby sister and I couldn't do anything.

"Are you okay?" Atticus asked.

"I am now," I answered.

Just as we finished shopping and got home around five in the afternoon I began to do some research. Finding out where he lives seemed like a goal, and then I'll go toward executing a plan. If I find that snippet of information and carefully continue this may just work. The idea I had at the time was to make it look as Alaina had runaway then we'll run. I was a woman on a dangerous, insane mission.

"Hey, what is up with you?" Atticus asked beginning to notice my new behavior.

"Nothing," I answered.

"Mallca ..."

"Don't Mallca me," I replied giving him the look that I usually would when I denied his push for an answer to what I am up too.

"What are you up to? Since I know you so well it is probably going to get either you or the both of us in trouble."

Then I had the thought of . . . why does he assume that it is going to be trouble? I know at times yes, my plans will involve trouble, but why does he every time go to that conclusion? He has trouble plans too, well, not when he's by himself. When he's with me he only gets worse. Anyway, Atticus was going to find out because I was going to need his assistance.

"I think I found Alaina. Remember that little girl we saw today at the store, I have the strongest belief that was her. The birthmark on her neck, the tracing of my scar, and she even knew my name before I ever said anything. Also when I said Alaina, she responded," I rambled. I knew that it was crazy, but all the pieces were falling into place.

"Are you sure?" he asked. For a minute there I had believed he doubted me, thinking I was crazy. Then I really looked. Atticus never doubted me, I knew what he was up to; he was making sure that I had believed in my suspicion myself.

"Yes I am."

I could not believe it when I finally found his location. He was right here all along and I had known nothing of it. Illingsworth's main housing was on the other side of town where, as I call it, the rich people live. Always had nice looking houses that seemed too big for one person to take care of themselves. Not to mention the fancy lawn statues such as gnomes or the occasional lion. I hoped that Alaina would not be corrupted by luxury, but I knew if she was truly a Siyas, there would be no chance of that happening.

Chapter
14

It was all nerve racking. I think by the time it was all over I did not have any nerves left to give. Every portion of my body and reasoning were contradicting each other. One was screaming to save her while the other was telling me not to. The possible consequences kept creeping its way back into my mind. I could be caught and given the death penalty, or worse . . . sent back to Prison 17-70. Yes, going back to that hell on Earth would be much worse than dying. If so I may as just jump from the truck and make it easier for myself. I knew the answer to my question . . . I had to try and save her. I was only going to involve one person in this mission, myself. I could not let Atticus take the pain with me for my foolishness. I knew then that this may be the last action I may ever take.

Looking through my closet I searched for something appropriate to wear. It had to be basic and easy to move. I found what I was looking for. I figured jeans would be fine and I just put on a black long sleeved under shirt. My eyes wandered toward a blue jean jacket, but I was trying to be sneaking, not stylish. Considering that all my hoodies had some kind of identification written on them, they were out of the question. However, I remember that Atticus may a few and I found a black hoodie that kind of looked big on me, but fit nicely. I then grabbed my grey and blue sneakers. I can run in any kind of shoes with backs unless they are flats or high heels. What I had believed, for the last time, I sat on our bed contemplating with my thoughts.

As usual I tried to talk myself out of it, but nothing seemed to work. My will to do this was too strong and the only way to stop me would be to take my last breath. Knowing myself, being very stubborn, I would find a way to complete it from the grave. I thought nothing could stop me.

"Mallca?" a familiar voice said in the doorway. I turned my head to see Atticus.

"Atticus . . ." I answered.

"I'm going with you," he told me.

Atticus doesn't really know the extent of what he means to me and how dangerous this would be. He and Alaina are my whole world and are the only people I can show emotion to. That this could very well be the last time I will ever see him and I want it to be a joyous memory. He was not surprised when I answered, "No."

"I figured you would say that, but I may as well try," he said. I felt as he thought I was mad at him or I didn't trust him. More likely it was that he probably thought that I thought he would just get in my way. No, I never thought any of that.

"It's not that I do not want you there with me . . . it's just that, think about it with two people . . . okay, I care too much about you to allow you to be in any danger." I finally came out with giving him a kiss before heading toward the door.

"Mallca . . ." I heard from behind.

"You can't talk me out of it . . ." I said turning around meeting his lips once again. Atticus kissing me was a lot different than me kissing him. He always had a deeper passion than I did. I just wanted to stay there with him and be like this forever. I could feel the connection between us as we were always meant to be, from the day we met. I just melted, but I quickly regained myself. We then broke off and put our heads together.

"Nice try," I responded.

"That's not what it means." He replied.

"What?"

"Good luck and I love you."

I showed him one last smile and rushed out of the house.

I took my bike and ended up locking it up about a half mile down the street at a local restaurant. The walk there did me good to become loose and clear headed. I was going to need it for better judgment. The house wasn't hard to find as I looked it up to see what it actually looked like, also I memorized the address, and I knew Illingsworth would have the biggest white house on the block. If that did not say Illingsworth, I don't what did. Knowing that gates would be both locked and guarded I went around to the sides. Of course, the challenge got harder as stone walls blocked my way. I swore the man made the wall like the Great Wall of China. It was pointless to even attempt to climb it bare handed. To my advantage there was a large tree next to it that had branches that went over the wall into the yard. Lucky for me, climbing trees was and still is mine and Atticus's favorite outdoor activity. So of course I was a natural at it. Like a monkey I scurried up to cross the only branch large enough to hold me, and it looked barely enough. I took my time crossing over, but my luck ran out when I reached the other side of the wall; the stupid branch broke. I slammed against the ground and it seemed I was not majorly injured just bruised. I whispered "ouch" to myself before getting up and slowly making my way around the house.

Everything seemed quiet and normal for a psychotic man, his backyard had a pool and a child's play set. Well, at least I knew Alaina was being taken care of and not a prisoner. I looked up to see a balcony with pink curtains. When I looked at the room I knew two things, I knew that was the room I wanted and I would have to change Alaina's mind about the color pink. Next to the balcony was a rose ivy wall that I could easily use as a ladder to get up to the top. So I began to ascend. As I was half way up I heard the back door open. Out stepped a maid with a dog.

'What an ugly and cute little thing . . .' I thought to myself.

The dog was a toy poodle and I am not a fan of the curls so by my own discomfort of course I would not like the dog. I am more of a German Shepard or Samoa type of person. I like the medium to large dogs. By the fact the dog is child friendly it probably belongs to Alaina and if she thinks it is cute, I do too. The fur ball could grow on me . . . maybe.

Quickly I figured I could get farther up to avoid detection so I began climbing again, but I lost my footing. I slipped grabbing tightly on. I could feel some of the thorns piercing my hands as I was no longer careful what I grabbed. The bushes begun to make ruffling noises and the dog reacted by growling. The little dog already knew that I didn't like...how funny. I quickly regain composure and hugged the wall to escape sight. Lucky me for wearing black at night and being this high up as I blended in as a shadow off the tree.

"Oh, I bet it's just a squirrel, and you don't need to get it," she said, "Come on, Kamva."

As they were going inside I got my footing back and calmed my fast pumping heart. Before I continued I thought about what the maid had called the dog, Kamva. If this was Alaina's dog it had to have a significant meaning to it. Then I figured it out, it was in the letters of the dog's name.

K is for Kenari, our mother.

A is for Arrington, our father.

M is for Mallca, me.

V is for Vaughan, our brother.

A is for Alaina, that would be her.

She named the dog by adding the first letter of the Siyas's family together, our family. I was sure I could to like the dog with a name like that.

Finally I arrived at the top of the wall and I carefully went over the railing. I was scared that I could fall, because I would be discovered, broken, or dead, perhaps all three. Well, it wasn't my only fear as Alaina wouldn't remember me or she had been turned against me. I tip toed to the door and listened in as well as looked.

There she was, in that room was a little dirty blonde girl that was my little sister. She sat on her pink bed in her pajamas playing with dolls. Instead of playing it seemed more like talking to them.

"You just would not believe it. I saw Mallca," she explained, "I dream of this day since I go. I know she comes."

I heard every word she said even if she doesn't have correct grammar yet, but she is like four so it seems acceptable. I decided to make her wish come true and I knew she had waited for this moment. I softly knocked so only she could have heard it and entered.

"Who?" she asked.

"Me. It's Mallca." I said showing my face.

"No! You no Mallca!" she cried running across the room toward the closet. If it was me I would have gone for the door, but something told me she believed me, just did not want to or couldn't.

"Yes it is. Just look at my face and tell me that I am not your big sister." I pleaded moving closer to her and keeping my distance by sitting on the bed.

It took a couple minutes for her to even come closer to me. She cautiously climbed on and got close to my face. She was looking for the only proof that she knew that could tell that it was actually me. I was only one hundred percent sure of one way to have her fully convinced. I turned my face and she got a view of the scar. Like every time she sees it she is hypnotized to touch it and trace it.

"It really is you!" she squealed with delight as she wrapped her arms around my neck embracing me. We had both been waiting this for such a long time. Right there I had wanted to twirl her around and run straight out of there never looking back.

"I told them that you were coming to get me, but they did not believe a word I said," she announced releasing me from the hold.

"Who didn't believe you?" I questioned getting scared that she had told someone that could tell Illingsworth that I had come. He would have locked me up faster than I could escape. Even if I did escape I'm sure he'd come after me.

"Them." Alaina pointed to her stuffed animals, mainly one of a pink dog. I was relieved instantly by this fact. "I told Kamva. Who he gonna tell?"

I smiled at her as she said that and suddenly began packing some of her toys and clothes into a bag. She must have known that I was taking her with me. I had to help her with basically all of it because as a four year old just only wanted to take toys and barely any clothing. Only a few were allowed as she needed to be quick and we did not have enough time to pack the child's entire bedroom. We were within seconds of leaving when a knock was heard at the door. Quickly I dove under the small bed which was almost not big enough underneath for me to fit. It was a tight squeeze for me. Without me saying anything Alaina pulled down the comforter to the floor to hide under the bed. Someone would have to move it to see me. I was convinced then that she believed me about who I was.

"Yes?" Alaina asked inviting the person at the door to come in.

"Your father wishes to speak with you right now miss," the maid said. It was a different one than before. I actually gaged at the earful of what she said about Illingsworth being Alaina's father. He was nowhere near to be called her father. Alaina's father was Arrington Siyas, and he was my father too.

"Now?" she questioned. I could tell any other time she would have gone, but because of me she was hesitant.

"Yes, he said now." She repeated herself.

"Okay," she answered, "I'll be right back." She whispered the last part toward her stuff animals that happened to be piled up on the on top of the bed, but I knew she was talking to me. She then left with the maid and I silently waited for her return . . .

Illingsworth's study was only down the long hallway from Alaina's room. The floor boards creaked with every step by the maid as Alaina was not heavy enough to cause them to creak unless she jumped. When at the door an eerie feeling and cold chill could be felt. The maid knocked on the door and a stern voice told them to come in. Illingsworth was sitting in his chair viewing some of the apparent "business" papers that lay upon the desk. He then folded one up and placed it inside his sleeve as he would need it for later.

"I brought her as you requested sir," the maid announced. "Thank you, you may leave," he commanded. She quickly left the room and closed the door.

"You need to see me." Alaina said.

"Yes. How are you?" he asked. She had not have been with the crazy nut of a man very long, but even she knew that this was weird for him to ask her randomly at night when they spoke at dinner only roughly two hours before.

Like any child I have known she answered, "Fine."

"I called you down before bedtime to ask you a question my dear," he stated making Alaina very nervous as she had never been in this kind of situation before now, it was as if her was interrogating her.

"Okay?" she said showing her becoming scared of him.

"How is your sister, Mallca is it?" he asked. Alaina jumped by his question and happen to see a small metal object shift under the papers.

'How long has it been since she left? What could Illingsworth want that could take so long?' I thought to myself while still cramped underneath the bed. Different ideas of what could be happening flash in and out of my mind. They ventured from the casual talk to him actually questioning her that he knows I am here. During this time and I do not remember why I had kept my cellphone on vibrate. Instead of a house phone Atticus and I used cells that were actually provided by his mom, lucky us. Also oddly enough it began to go off and I thought 'who could that be?' I knew Atticus knew better than to text me as he knows what I am actually doing. Sometimes I wished I never looked at my phone:

To: Me
From: Unknown Number
 Message: I know you are here Mallca. Come on and visit me in my study down the hall from your location. I know both Alaina and I would like that, to see you one more time.

'That bastard', I thought what seemed fitting at the time. He has Alaina and he knows that I am here. He probably scared the poor girl into telling him or he had known all along and needed her to confirm his suspicions. That was why he wanted to see her earlier. I had to go and get her, but is he going to use her against me like any crazy mad man? It did not matter, I had to save her.

Slowly I got out from underneath the bed by taking a few scratches on my back from the boards being so low. I went to the door and looked to see if the coast was clear. I don't know why he knew I was there and probably told everyone not to touch me as I was his problem to handle. Like with the maid the floor boards creaked under my every step as I headed toward my unknown fate. This was not the first time I had gone through this walk to fate. About three times in the last five years. Five years ago when I received my Predetermine, then a year after when I was going inside the prison, and the day I got out returning to the real world. This was going to be no different than the rest.

The floor boards at the end of the hallway were better constructed than the rest of them. Probably so he can hear people coming, but not coming in. He knew I was coming anyway so being quiet was not really an issue. I admit it was me stalling for time.

Pictures of the Illingsworth before him were nailed up on the walls. There was him, his father, and then the bastard that started this entire deal with the Predetermine. This was his grandfather Rodney Illingsworth. From what I understand he had received a position of power and believed he could make the world a better place if he controlled what the people actually did with their lives. Of course some people revolted and that was where the prisons numbered from 17-00 to 17-99 come from. Ninety-nine of these hells on Earth places exist and people are forced to run them, even if they do not want to. Hopefully this madness stops at Terreagan. A light knock came to the door when I finally arrived. If I had been raised any different I would not have knocked and just barged right on in like I would do to any other closed door. However, this was not my house and I wasn't raised differently.

"Enter Mallca." Illingsworth said from the other side. It was weird he knew that it was me and not a maid. Like I had said, he probably ordered everyone away. I entered with a stern face showing that I was not scared of what he could have done to me. "How good it is to see you again. What has it been like five years? My, you've grown up and quite nicely."

"You cannot even see me," I growled observing that he was turned around looking out the window.

"That is true. I guess the schooling did help, but you are too smart for that." I knew that it was him that sent Atticus and I back to school delaying me from doing anything.

"Yeah, and I am so smart that I cannot understand delusional and mad people when they talk," I said getting lippy as my father called it. I thought that Alaina was hidden out of harm's way and if I knew not I would not have said it.

"That was not nice. Did you parents ever teach not call people names? Also don't you have set an example for your little sister?" Illingsworth said turning around in his chair. I gasped at the sight of Illingsworth having Alaina tightly gripped on the shoulder with small gun to her head. How could he have done such a thing to a little girl?

"Let her go!" I screamed.

"I don't think so," he replied. Every muscle in my body told me to charge him, but not with Alaina at sake. "I figured that we would have a chat before I call security and have you arrested. Sit down, will you?"

"I'd rather stand."

"Your choice, but you could be there a while," he replied trying to avoid the topic of our conversation, "You have answers that I want and same for me. I have answers to your unlimited amount of questions."

Damn, he had known about everything.

"Okay then, why? Why take Alaina? Why come to my Predetermine?" I asked knowing I could stand here the rest of my time asking questions and never get answers.

"Aren't we jumping the gun? I believe it would be best if tell you my story and then still see if you have questions. You may not seem inclined to listen as you like straight to the point, but I think most of the answers you are searching for are here. You see, I have a Predetermine to follow as well."

Why would he have one? He made more questions than answering them. "To continue the Predetermine for me is to continue the Predetermine as my father did, not to marry, but never be alone, determine one child's Predetermine, and just may make the Breaker. My grandfather started this all to protect the one he loved, but look where that got us. Alaina is one of my ways to never be alone as she was a poor child stuck in chaos and you are the child who I had a hand to determine. Also I chose you to be the Breaker if you could really do it. I looked for ages after I took control to find the right one. I found your name in the list of your month and you name screamed at me as did another child's, but yours seemed to cry the loudest. However, I guess I got an Issigna either way unlike my grandfather. The last five years of your life have been set-up to play out as you see it. Minor complications here and there, but all this is your Predetermine!"

'What the hell was the guy talking about?' I thought. I was really confused. As I said before only to repeat myself as this left more questions and only answered a few. He did answer the two I had asked out loud.

"What is the Breaker?" I asked. I had an idea, but I wanted to be sure.

"The Breaker is the one person who stops the Predetermine or what most of you know as people who break the rules. The only person with a strong enough will to actually do something about it. They break not only their Predetermine and set a new one, but break the actual idea of Predetermine."

It was exactly what I thought the Breaker was.

"Why do you even have the Breaker? Can't you just stop it yourself?" I asked.

"Why not have someone? If I just ended it would disrupt the grand design of it all and everything that we Illingsworths' have put forward. You don't understand the reasons and they will finally die," he explained. Okay, then all my suspicions of him being nuts and having a mental illness were confirmed to be true. He seemed glad that this was all happening. He began laugh like he was mad, and not the angry kind.

"You said my life was set-up," I said getting his attention. I had to keep him focused or he could hurt, even kill Alaina. All I needed was to keep him talking until I could find a way to free Alaina.

"You had to be tempted to break your Predetermine for me to be sure. The wyvern, punishment, jobs, all that happened by no accident. You coming down sick with diphtheria was an unexpected accident that brings forth the Predetermine into a reality, but it proved to me you were strong enough."

"You were watching me the entire time and pissed me off for a reason?" I inquired.

"In theory, yes, all Predetermines are linked to one another by no accident. Like I said it is the grand design."

He was telling me everything like I was going to be writing the history books . . . damn, that is why my predetermined job is to be an archeologist. I am discovering the truth and sharing it with the world. For once he was right. Why go through all the trouble? And what will happen to him? Not that I had cared or anything.

"I don't quite follow."

"You are the Breaker Mallca Siyas, the challenger of the Predetermine! I saw you as a person I could push enough to do something about it."

He was a sick human being, if that is even the correct terms to use without getting my mouth washed out with soap. This was a chess game where he was the king and I am either the knight or the queen. The mansion was the rook that I took out and I came for the kill. Or the Predetermine was the dragon and I am its slayer.

Which way it is, it is all the same. Only one of us was to be the victor. Now that I actually think about Illingsworth is only a pawn in our game; the real king is the Predetermine. The Predetermine was feeding off power-hungry delusional people who think they are doing this for greater good. It was controlling everyone since the day it was created and needed someone to say "checkmate".

"Doesn't that help your troubled mind?" he asked. I nodded.

"Now my final question," I asked. He raised an eyebrow thinking what else I could have left to ask him. "What are we to do now?" As he said that it should end, it did. Let's say it did end there in the form of a three year old.

Alaina seemed to be tired of the waiting and talking of the adults. With her pearly white teeth she bit down on Illingsworth's hand. He cried out in pain as I swore she broke skin to reveal blood. To get to release him he tossed her to the floor. Her body and head gave a nasty thud when she hit the floor. I saw this as my chance.

"Alaina!" I said as I watched her fall and I leaped into action.

Time then moved so slow, but all so fast.

I found myself running toward him at full speed and strength.

He barely had enough time to react as he raised his weapon. We were both standing at a close distance where it did not take long for me to reach him. He got off one bullet before I slammed with palms forward. As he fell backwards a piece of paper fell from his sleeve to the floor and he went straight out the window. Everything followed him out the window, the glass, the curtains, and even me. I happened to catch myself before I followed in descending to the ground. It wasn't toppling over that hurt, it was what I caught myself on which was the window seal which still had glass. The glass still left in the window pierced into my hands and it didn't help that they were already pierced by the thorns. Fortunately I was still functional enough to pull myself back up to the room. I just decided to lay there, tired and hurt.

"Mallca!" Alaina said coming over to me. I was at ease knowing Illingsworth had not hurt her in the fall. She hugged me with a much stronger force than when I had first seen her earlier. I returned the hug with my wrist as I saw that my hands had both figurative and literal had blood on them. I finally had Alaina back with me. At my feet I saw a letter with my name written on it. I attempted to pick it up, but Alaina had to do because of my hands. She unfolded it and showed it to me to read:

Mallca,

I see that my choice in you was correct in choosing you to be the Breaker. With me now dead, the Predetermine is over. You have released the curse on the world and within me as I had a multiple personality. For that I thank you, for all that you have done and given up in your life. I have no way to repay you. I will explain everything to the people as I have put everything on the bottom of the letter. Take pride in the life you can now have, living it how you want to.

Illingsworth

I was completely speechless by his letter to me. I read the bottom of the letter and he was right that it explained everything or at least gave instructions to find out everything. Even if they did not believe they had to face the fact and believe there was no one left with enough power to enforce the Predetermine.

When did he write this to me?
How did he know that this would end this way?

Again I had questions, but I was able to answer them myself. Inside the actual Terreagan Illingsworth was a sane man that knew the Predetermine would end with me. He wrote the letter when he had the chance. Taking Alaina he knew that it would bring me here that night to stop it. I then decided to finally look out the shattered window down below.

I saw an image that would ever escape from my memories. It could have been him getting up or lying there broken and bloody on the ground. It had been the second scenario. Either way, one status of life was correct. It was life and death; Illingsworth was death and I was life.

Chapter

15

It was not how I had planned it to end. I also could not
believe that I had done it by sin, killing a man with my
two bare hands. Of course they were not bare then, but it
was my blood. As I said it was his blood too as I had killed him.
I looked at my hands to see wounds re-opened and new ones
emerging. Now they will match my face and back. I guessed this
was a way to remember the Predetermine, to make sure at least one
person in the world would never forget.

I never allowed Alaina to see out the window as soon as some
of my strength returned we headed out the door. She had been
through enough already and did not need to add the sight of a
dead guy her sister killed. It was best to keep it unknown to her or
until she asked. At least I hope she wouldn't.

Before we actually left the house I made a stop by the
bathroom to find the medical kit. Oddly the house was empty, but
I didn't think of anything of it. I grabbed the gauze and medical
tape to wrap my hands. Lucky there was enough to use for both
hands.

Cleaning my cuts with the water made them sting the dirt and blood cleared out, but it was the only way to stop an infection and better access my injuries. My palms looked as they were ruined. I knew that I was going to have odd palm marks that were unique. Placing the bandage on first I winced at the pain as Alaina waited outside. I would not let her see. She'd probably ask questions. I wrapped them in the gauze and placed medical tape around it. I looked at my handy work, pun included...it was not professional, but decent.

Alaina grabbed the bag we packed from her room and met me by the stairs. Before we left I checked the bag to make sure she didn't add anything she didn't need. We could return later for what she had left behind. She was, in a way, ready to go. We walked to the door as she held my fingers as much as I could handle. I knew both of us really wanted her to hold my hand. Whichever way did not last long and neither did the time of relief because it was not over for me. It ended as we reached the doorway.

We tried to hang on to each other, but we were surrounded by the police department. All the red and blue lights flashed blinding anyone who looked inside. They must have been called and saw my actions of a murder and a kidnapping. Only which the first one is kind of true and the second is taking my family back. Alaina and I had the truth and they would not believe a criminal or take the word of a four year old. They could see it as I had corrupted her to lie to protect me.

"Go and tell them you want your brother-in-law, Atticus Issigna. You remember him?," I explained softly knowing there was no way out of this that ended in not leaving with the police. Alaina had the eyes to refuse to leave me, but a smile and a nod convinced her. Before leaving me she hugged me and told me she loved me. I did the same let her go. As she reached the officer I got on my knees and placed my hands on my head. I smirked as the grabbed my wrist and cuffed me.

"Let's go boys," I said smugly beginning to walk off on my own. The officers roughly pushed me forward and I took that as a sign to shut up. From what I could see of Alaina she giggled at me and I walked to the police car walking tall with my head held high instead of my tail between by legs.

It seemed like hours since I left to Atticus, but it was because it had been almost three. That doesn't seem very long, but of course he begins to worry for me. It was about eight o'clock at night when the phone rang. Atticus's heart skipped a beat seeing that it was the police department. He calmed himself before answering.

"Hello?" he asked. He hoped to hear my voice on the other line as he was my one phone call.

"Hello, is this Atticus Issigna?" the officer on the other line asked.

"Yes. Can I help you with something?"

"We are calling to inform you on two matters. We have a little girl here claiming to be your sister-in-law and are you aware of your wife's actions tonight?" he asked.

"No," Atticus lied. Well, he wasn't completely lying.

"Well, she has been arrested on the changes of kidnapping and murder." Atticus did not want to answer to the man's comment because he wanted to hear it from me.

"What's the girl's name?" Atticus asked making sure he was talking about Alaina.

"Alaina Illingsworth." He answered being told by Illingsworth's records. Atticus gaged for me about the incorrect name. The police knew nothing that Alaina had been kidnapped and that my family were the victims.

"Her last name is Siyas." Atticus corrected him.

"Excuse me?" he asked.

"Her real name is Alaina Kenari Siyas, born September 23rd in Prison 17-70." he explained.

"Well, can we please ask you to come down to the station? When you arrive ask for Officer Fawcetter."

"Alright, thank you for informing me. I'll be down right away," Atticus informed, "Good-bye."

They both hung up the phone and Atticus could not believe what he had just heard. Alaina was with the police and I was arrested. Well, a part of him could believe that I had been arrested. He joked that I was most likely to get arrested. When none of us got senior superlatives we decided to come up with our own. That was one he gave me, jokingly of course, well...not so much. Without a second thought Atticus grabbed his coat, wallet, and keys running out to the car and left.

When I arrived I had to empty my pockets and take off anything I was wearing. All I had with me was a little spare change, a necklace, my wedding ring, and the note from Illingsworth. Of course no one was nosey enough to read the note. If someone would have read the letter all that had happened would have been pointless and the changes could have been dropped. They were the least of my worries as I did not get a trial or jail time as I was sent straight back to Prison 17-70. My stomach dropped hearing that and I attempted to say something. However, all that I got was a hit and shutup. I was going back to my nightmares.

In the jail truck I was taken to familiar settings of the endless forest. The trucks emptied out and into the lines leading to the marking. This time the lines were shorter and I was all alone. Instead of being with the other so called criminals I was already loaded where the ones go after being marked. It was because I already had a mark. Still I could feel those people's pain when the hot metal is placed on their skin. As they all loaded into the pick-up truck everyone stared at me. I was the only one there not in any kind of pain. Thankfully because of the fewer amounts of people movement was allowed.

"What did you do?" I heard in this bartender kind of voice behind me.

"Me?" I asked turning around making sure that the woman was indeed talking to me. She nodded. "I have been here before for breaking my Predetermine. I wanted a different job and tried secretly to obtain it."

I revealed the wyvern to the woman who only seemed a few years older than me. She had light brown hair with green eyes.

"Didn't learn the first time, did ya?" she asked.

"No, I learned this is my sentence for my crimes. I seemed more appropriate to send me back here than to sit and die in jail. As you know, prison isn't any option as these prisons worl find for that role too," I explained.

"What?"

"I killed Terreagan Illingsworth." I said. Not something I should proud of, but inside I kind of smiled.

"No way you could have done that," She was shocked and her jaw dropped. I nodded to her telling her that I was not kidding.

"Rimdara," she introduced herself holding out her hand.

"Mallca," I answered carefully taking her hand. As she grasped my hand I winced as she took it and I could tell she was trembling. "Sorry I cut up my hands." I showed her my hands and she understood.

We arrived late at night and by the position of the moon I could tell it was around ten o'clock. I looked around seeing the place had not changed and neither did the people. Only been out less than a year and still my face was familiar, especially to Maurus.

"Mallca?" he whispered, "What are you doing here?"

"I killed him . . . Illingsworth. With him gone no one is left to enforce the Predetermine . . . this nonsense is over." I explained. Like Rimdara, Maurus was stunned by this fact.

"You sure?" he asked. I knew from one of our previous conversations he wanted this to end as much as I did.

"We just need to hold on just a little longer," I explained before leaving.

Again I was placed in the red barrack, same scarfs and jobs. Walking inside the barrack again flooded my mind with memories of the years my life that were wasted here. The bed where Alaina was born and my mother died. The spot on floor where I laid after being whipped and the bed I was in for not even ten minutes after. Bethany slept there before she died the same place I had almost bled to death. That sweet innocent girl that I had loved like a little sister. Oddly I had the same bed as before, the same one I had almost died in from diphtheria and became married to Atticus in.

I could tell my the position and the fact I had crafted my promise "keep safe" in the wood. At least Atticus wasn't here with me.

That morning going to breakfast, if you could call it that, I passed the same place where I held Vaughan in my arms when he died. Asking me what love was and I told him only what I knew. With all these emotional memories I almost broke down and cried. I knew that was not ideal because to them it shows a sign of weakness. That day must have been a day to regain old memories and friends, if you could call him a friend. That would be the last word I would have used to call Batson or I called Batson the Bastard.

At first I tried to hide my face from him, but that only works for so long because we had just been called for roll. Roll tells the guards who is still alive, dying, or dead. All we do is show our arms and we are checked off. Batson looks and calls as Romone checks them off. He was getting closer to me by the minute and just my luck as marks are never recycled unless the owner is dead. When they die it says the mark is reused next to it. Last time I had checked I wasn't dead...yet.

"Wyvern," Batson announced grabbing my arm with the same grip he has used before. I almost got away with it as I kept my head down showing the back of my head. "Wyvern . . ."

Batson's left hand swooped around and grabbed my cheek bones to turn my head to look. I stared right into his eyes. His index finger traced the scar on my jawbone which he had given me.

"Sir, what is it?" Romone asked because they had taken so long at one person.

"I thought that was you," he barked as he pulled me out throwing me against the ground. "What did ya do now or did ya miss me?"

I thought to myself to keep my hands down and not punch his lights out.

"Not likely," I answered. It was the best I could say, really.

"That's too bad," he answered, "So what did you break now?"

Funny how he said break and Illingsworth had called me the Breaker. Also I had broken a window to kill him.

"Can't we reminisce later?" I asked and not because I thought this was enjoyable. The newcomers, even the ones who never left knew that I had returned and retook my place as the only fear in Batson's eyes. "You have no higher president to take orders from."

"What are you talking about girl?" he asked. He either didn't know yet or he was playing stupid, which wasn't hard for him. He probably already knows about Illingsworth, but didn't know that I was the one who did it.

"She killed Illingsworth!" I heard Rimdara up the line as she was checked off before me as her symbol was a bear. Batson returned his glance to me and we stared at each other, but he was speechless.

"I. Know. Everything." I said to him separating each word with a sharp tongue. I expected to meet Batson's hand across my face again as it seemed like only option to retaliate against me. I received nothing. Our battle had risen again.

By the time Atticus arrived at the station I was already long gone. Alaina sat in a chair with cup of water in her hands. At first she didn't notice Atticus, but when he went by and she saw him her eyes became brighter. Before going to the desk he waved to her and of course she returned the gesture.

"Hi. I'm here to speak with an Officer Fawcetter." Atticus explained to the receptionist.

"Of course," she answered getting on the phone to find him. Minutes later a tall African American man with short hair came out.

"Atticus Issigna?"

"Officer Fawcetter?"

The two men exchanged greetings before he led Atticus to a private office to discuss the matters at hand.

"It seems you know much of Alaina here," he said hoping to get Atticus to tell how much he knew of Alaina. Atticus said it more like being interrogated without being in the room. I had spoken with the officer as well and knew he could be quite intimidating.

"Yes, she is my wife's little sister," he explained.

"Well, all we are asking is a way to prove that you are a relative," he asked.

"Alright, well, I am not blood related so that seems a little difficult for me to do. I know that she was born on September 23rd, in Prison 17-70 to Arrington and Kenari Siyas. She has two older siblings Mallca and Vaughan Siyas. Mallca is the only survivor. Alaina came from Kenari breaking her Predetermine. I am married to Mallca legally so that makes me family." Atticus explained. "The only ways I see that you can check my story is obtaining a blood test of both Mallca and Alaina and test it and find our marriage license or look up Kenari's records."

Officer Fawcetter did not know what else to ask for. It was obvious that Atticus knew the girl and knew what he was talking to prove he was at least related in some way. He had no way to deny it.

"Can you wait here? I'll be right back." He asked.

"What about Mallca?" Atticus asked.

"Right now we are focused on Alaina."

It seemed like hours, but it was only an hour before he actually returned with papers and Alaina.

"Atticus!" she said running from the officer straight to Atticus.

"Are you okay?" he asked.

"They poke me and it hurt," she replied showing him the bandage on her arm.

"What did you do to her?" Atticus asked unsure if he should getting upset at this moment.

"Before Mrs. Siyas-Issigna left the station we took a blood sample just in case and we just tested it against one from Alaina. They both match in records to Kenari Siyas as siblings so it checks out that you are indeed Alaina's brother-in-law so we are releasing her to you." Fawcetter explained.

"Thank you." Atticus replied.

"With that settled the kidnapping charge on Mrs. Siyas-Issigna may be dropped, however, the other charge still stands as is. Do these items look familiar to you?" he asked placing an evidence bag out containing the items they had collected from me earlier.

"Yes, that's the necklace she always wears and this is our wedding ring," he explained showing the one he was wearing on his finger. "Where is she?"

"Due to the fact it was Terreagan Illingsworth she had murdered she has been sent to Prison 17-70. I recall you know the area?" Atticus nodded. He was not about to get into an argument about me or himself. That could have jeopardized my chances. He makes a pretty good defense in the fact he would have asked if they knew I did it or not. Just because I was in the house doesn't mean anything. The real killer could have jumped out the window.

"What is the folded piece of paper?" Atticus asked changing the subject off the prison. Not only that he sure that was not something I had when I left earlier.

"We are not actually sure. No one has come in to inspect it yet. Assuming that she may have known she would be caught she may have written it as a good-bye letter to you. I can get a pair of gloves and you may read it." Fawcetter said. Atticus knew that I don't write notes anymore since we are out of school and plus we had said our good-byes earlier.

"Thank you and I think I will," Atticus replied. Officer Fawcetter then left the room returning moments later with large pair latex gloves. Atticus quickly slipped them on before removing the note from the bag. He wondered what was written on this piece of paper as he knew good-bye was not one of the words. He turned the note around to see if anything was written on the outside and there was a name . . . Mallca. He thought it was odd that I would have written a note to myself if it was believed to be addressed to him. Also as he opened to view the contents he realized that the handwriting was different. He was fully positive the note was for me and not written by me as he read through it. Carefully reading every word and sentence to make sure he knew what Illingsworth was talking about and he even read it twice.

"This isn't for me," Atticus informed as Officer Fawcetter's face went to a puzzled look. "This note is addressed to Mallca from Illingsworth. I believe that you guys are the ones that should be reading this, not me."

Atticus smiled as the words left his mouth and handed the note over. He understood what was written on the note and what it then meant. The madness was over.

Officer Fawcetter read the letter over again as Atticus had, but it took him longer as Atticus believed he read the note over three times. His eyes just continued to go back and forth. When he finished he did not wait for any comment before rushing out to the chief. Atticus swore he heard him scream "It's over!"

"Is this true?" the Chief asked. Neither if the two could have believed what they had just heard and only thought that it could be a hoax. The matched the handwriting and did any test to see if this could be a trick by seeing if there was evidence of erase marks, trembling in the words, or any possible secret messages. They had tested for fingerprints only to find the only people that could have ever touched the note who were me, Illingsworth, and Alaina. At first they had a suspicion that I had tampered with it, but how could I? I read it and it was addressed to me. This only meant one thing, the Predetermine was really over.

As the note was cleared to be true, which took about two days, it was announced across the country that no longer we had guidelines to follow. People that were locked away in the prisons that no longer had crimes against them to keep them there were to be released as soon as possible. At first I was not sure that I would have my freedom, but, in all, I did technically break my Predetermine again. Since I was to be an archeologist I could no longer complete my job since I was told I would probably be in here for quite some time. I guess it was either this reason the Committee saw or the fact I freed the country. For the news to reach the prison heads took about two more days. As I said the people were to be released and the prisons were to be destroyed. They could be either destroyed completely from existence or made into memorials for the people who died and serve as a part of our history. It was also said different facilities would be built to accommodate criminals who broke the new laws. The marks were now as symbols of the cruelty, knowing the people who suffered, and the believers that one day this was possible. Of course the people who had jobs because of the Predetermine lost them, but I think they were okay with it. They banded together to create a new government. Their was only one last job on Atticus's honey to do list: come and get me.

"Go get Mallca?" Alaina asked as they were starting the drive to where they were informed to get me.

"Yeah, we're going to bring her home where she belongs," he replied smiling back at her in her seat. She returned the gestures tightly hugging the stuffed animal of a dragon. Atticus bought it for her the day after he was given custody of her. He was at the market and she fell in love with it. Alaina told him it reminded her of me.

Atticus could still not believe they had actually sent me back to Prison 17-70. He thought the prisons were for only people that break their Predetermines, not for suspected killers. Atticus had come up with a better explanation than I did. Illingsworth was the Predetermine and I broke it. Make sense in my book so sure.

He remembered what this place had done to me the first time, left me with scars and terrible nightmares. What good comes out of these? Absolutely nothing at all and that was four years, instead of a week. However, I had been here before and was a familiar face so those days can be like years that turn into a lifetime. Atticus only hoped that the damage wasn't already done.

Chapter

16

The drive to the edge of Prison 17-70, the location Atticus was given to pick me up at, seemed like hours of joy and sorrow. Like I had at one time, Atticus had flashbacks about the four years he spent there. Even before arriving when we all sat in the back of the truck and Bethany had her head lying on his leg. If none of this ever existed and she would still be alive. However, Daphnia's fate would still be the same, but at least he would have had his sister.

Even though he lost them he at least had not lost me. I was the girl down the road, his best friend, who he had fallen in love with, and eventually married. I wondered sometimes without the Predetermine would have we gotten together. I guess that was the one only good thing it did. If not he probably either have bucked up and asked me or still be silently crushing on me behind my back with me still being clueless. For all I know I could dating Severn if not. So I guess I have to thank Predetermine for that; I feel I should be washing my mouth out. Just because it got Atticus and I together does not mean I will forgive all the other sins it has committed. For right then I had put it all behind me as I saw the familiar car approaching, too bad it was not Atticus.

"Thank you Mallca," I heard spoken behind me. It was Maurus as he sits down with me I wait for the first ride home to end.

"Thank me for what?" I asked.

"Saving us," he answered.

"No, I should be really thanking you. When I was here the first time you kept me alive. You helped when no one else would, cleaning and bandaging my gashes when I was whipped. Not to mention helping Atticus obtain the penicillin when I had diphtheria. Also I heard you were prepared when I had a reaction," I explained with as much gratitude I could.

"Okay, I get it and your welcome," he said stopping my rant of it being the other way around. Maurus was the person that kept me alive so in turn I could end it. By the time we had arrived at the edge people were already there for their family. As I was about to get off I saw a familiar couple of people getting out of a car.

"Good-bye Maurus. Good luck," I said hugging him before leaving him to go our separate ways.

"Good-bye Mallca. Please take care of yourself because I can't come and save you anymore," he hugged back before going with a friendly wave. I wished he would have stayed a little longer so I could hit for the comment.

Through the crowd of people I could see Atticus's head above the crowd, it was good that he is tall. Underneath I could probably see Alaina's tiny toddler shoes. Just when I was about to go find my family I hear my name, it was Rimdara.

"Yeah," I questioned before she hugged me out of the blue.

"Thank you so much," she said, "I want you to meet someone before you go. Come here."

A little boy around Alaina's again came running up into Rimdara's arms and it looked as neither of them could let go of each other. While at Prison 17-70 I learned Rimdara was twenty-three years old being five years older than me.

"Who is this?" I asked. Being the older sibling of a small child was something I thought of. I was eighteen and Alaina was three, I did not see the big deal. My gut had been telling my otherwise.

"This is my son Mitchel. Thanks to you he can grow up with his mommy," she explained. My gut had been right about him being her son. I never got to answer her as I heard my name being called again and felt someone wrap around my legs.

"Alaina!" I cried scooping her up in my arms tightly in a hug. Seconds later I propped her on my hip.

"Is this your daughter?" Rimdara asked. I never told her that I had a little sister as we were in separate areas.

"No," I laughed, "this is my little sister."

"Oh, I feel rude implying that to you, I'm sorry," she apologized.

"No its fine," I laughed again, "I thought Mitchel was brother so I guess we're even."

Now someone else was touching me in a familiar fashion. An arm came around my right side and a chin on the crook of my shoulder blade. Also there was snuggling into my neck. I knew who it was. Who else could have it been? Atticus was behind me and I turned right into his kiss. I had missed this.

"No guessing this your husband," she implied as I smiled and nodded, "Please keep in touch dear."

"Sure."

"How are you beautiful?" Atticus asked. I hate it when he uses pet names and he knows it. He's trying to be cute.

"Better now that you're here." I figured I'd throw him a bone.

With that we went on our separate ways. Rimdara and I did keep in touch and Alaina and her son became good friends. I joked that it could be another Atticus and me. I thought afterwards all this would simply blow over and only be the past, only repressed memories that I locked away deep in my subconscious, but that was not the case.

It had been about three weeks since the Predetermine and of course it all comes back to bite me. Alaina and I were playing in the living room while Atticus finished dinner. To be honest I was raising Alaina, more like we were her parents and her siblings. Recently I was bored and had just showed her how interesting and funny it was to blow your cheeks out and then push them back in so the air blows out. Innocent the game may seem, but in seconds anything can be a nightmare. One last time I did it and used my entire hands, and Alaina thought it would be funny to do so too.

I never told anyone what happened during my short stay at Prison 17-70. Like I said before, the week felt like years. Everyday Batson, who happened to go off the grid, would hit me for no apparent reason or he would find one. Word got around that Illingsworth had died so people were getting antsy. They thought it would be smart and attempt another escape, like I had made Vaughan go through. Again, if I hadn't, he would be here, and everyone tells me that I don't know that. Anyway, it ended in the same result; the guards having a shootout. People died, and I stayed inside hiding, and yet I was for blamed. It was almost worse the second time. I'll let the mind wonder for that.

The slap came so unexpected that I didn't have the time to defend myself. With her small hand she had enough strength and forces to knock the air of me. It felt like she hit me with a kicked kickball to the face. I was not sure at first what got into me, but when she smacked me I went to the floor. Everything started to flow back into my mind and memories exploded into view.

"No! I didn't do anything!" I screamed trying to escape my attacker that only seemed like a mirage of Alaina trying to fool me.

Upon hearing my screams stopped Atticus in his tracks and run to the living room to the commotion. He was startled by what he saw, me in the fetal position while Alaina stood about two feet away confused and about to cry. Tears welded up in her eyes because she could not understand what was going on and believed it to be her fault. Partly it was and neither of us knew what was going on either.

"What happened? You two alright?" he asked. Atticus was not sure what to do. More likely the question was, who to comfort? It was either the scared little girl or his terrified wife.

"What wrong Mallca?" Alaina sniffled. Atticus got his answer as he came to my side. Alaina was fine and it was me he had to worry about.

"Mallca, are you okay?"

It took a minute for me to realize that no one was going to hurt me if I calmed down. However, my breathing was still labored. It felt as if I was going to have a small anxiety attack. I moved to a sitting position and Atticus sat beside me placing his hand on my shoulder. Alaina saw that everything was fine and cautiously came over and hugged me before sitting down in my lap.

"Sorry Mallca," she apologized.

"You just shocked me that was all," I reassured her, "I'm going to bed; I'm kind of tired. You can leave some dinner in the fridge, night." I moved Alaina to the couch and headed for the stairs and as I passed the kitchen my nose begun to burn. "Hey Atticus, I think dinner is burning and just forget leaving any out if it is."

"Oh crap!" Atticus said running into the kitchen and turning off the stove. I smiled before jogging up the steps to our bedroom.

Turning on the lights seemed pointless so I just took off my shoes and slid under the covers into bed.

I couldn't move. Why wouldn't my feet and legs work? I was frozen in the position as I started to feel a smack against my back that only continued to get stronger. Of course this could only be accomplished by Batson and the other guards. I can feel slashes and bruises begin to appear and become deeper with every blow. I think I would have internal damage. Why would they be torturing me when this is all over? Before my eyes I saw the guards I have come to know with their favorite weapons of pain toward people that I know. There was Rimdara, Maurus . . . Atticus . . . not her, Alaina. Some of the guards had guns and I heard the triggers being pulled as if they were right next to my ears. If that was the case it would have explain the deafening ringing in them. Not only that, my hands burned like if I were the one of the ones that pulled the trigger on the people I cared about. I heard their screams and soon enough they died away. Why do I feel like I'm burning inside my head? I have movement in hands and I place them on my head. I am greeted with a wet feeling I assume that it is sweat until I bring them down to look at. I saw crimson red as I knew that it was my blood.

Outside of that dream I tossed and turned like a in violent outburst. I am drenched in my own cold sweat. I had to get away as I flailed my arms, but I wouldn't move. During that time I must have either woke Atticus with either smacking him or the tossing. He saw me hide deeply under the covers to escape something that I am unable to. Again I woke up in my screams and Atticus calling my name.

"Mallca, wake up!" he yelled repeatedly until I woke up with my arms grabbing hold of him forcing him to hold me. "Are you sure you're okay?"

I had no idea what to tell him because I was not so sure myself. I thought about lying to him, but I ended in telling him the truth.

"I don't know." I answered. Reluctantly I did fall back asleep with Atticus there holding me. Again with him there the nightmares did not return. He is like my dream catcher.

The next morning the sun shone in down in my face waking me from the pleasant slumber that I had just had. Actually what had fully aroused me was the alarm clock blaring at me. It read seven in the morning I had jumped out of bed knowing that I had to get Alaina ready for pre-school. I first expected to see Atticus still asleep when I noticed he was not there.

'Where could he be?' I thought to myself, 'He's never up this early.'

Getting out of bed I slipped on my slippers I heard voices down the hall in Alaina's room. I knew that something was not right because that child was never up until I went to get her up. I probed my head into the door to see what was going on. Atticus was showing Alaina varies outfits and of course she kept turning the poor guy down. I smiled and thought about standing there to just enjoy the moment, but I decided to intervene. I finally walked in grabbing a pair of sparkly jeans and a cute top, with a small jacket. I held it up showing it to her and she grinned.

"Yes," she agreed.

"Finally!" Atticus huffed as we laughed. It seemed he had been at this a while, "Morning."

"Morning," I yawned in return with my words handing over the outfit to Alaina.

We then walked down stairs to prepare for our days. Of course that meant breakfast and it was my turn. Thankfully my non-existent cooking skills were never really called upon in the morning unless it was for a special occasion such as a birthday or holiday.

"Don't forget that we have the meeting today at her school to talk about moving to the next grade," Atticus reminded.

"I won't," I groaned, "Alaina, breakfast!"

Just as I called her she came walking down the stairs going straight to the table. In the morning Alaina usually just wants a bowl of her favorite cereal which is fine. It is easy enough to grab a bowl, put some cereal in it, and some milk. If it had been anything else I may have been screwed because I usually can't cook anything without burning it unless it has directions and sometimes I don't even follow those. Lucky I picked up a few tricks while in school to help me out so I am not totally useless in the kitchen. As we sat waiting for Alaina's bus I noticed that Atticus kept looking over in my direction. I can always tell that he is hiding something.

"What is it?" I asked.

"What's what?" he mimicked except by adding and replacing some words.

"You are hiding something from me, I can always tell," I replied giving him my signature look of the deep stare. I would of bet or guessed that he had forgot that it was still me and I know my old ways still have him whipped.

"Okay, I called this morning and set you up a doctor appointment today at noon," he confessed.

"What?" I growled.

"I'm sorry, but I am just so worried about you and I love you. I cannot see you I pain. So please . . ." he pleaded. I cannot stand the begging and he did say he loved me. Those three words usually get me to agree to do about anything. I just melt and cannot believe that someone actually loves me.

"Fine," I agreed.

"Thank you," he said.

"Bye Mallca! Bye Atticus!" Alaina said as she flew out of the house and hurried to the bus.

"Bye Alaina," I said as the door closed.

It may have only been seven-thirty, but the time for us to leave and noon came too quickly. All I did before that was sit around and usually contemplate what I am going to do next. Atticus did not even dare to speak to me until it was time for us to leave and even I was trouble to go the car as I procrastinated. It did not matter because I knew this would be over soon and the doctor would probably tell me nothing was wrong. Also we were cut on time as we had to back home by three to meet Alaina home.

The doctor's office was how I expected. It was full of sick people and had the sanitized smell. After we checked in I found an area far away from the other people, but that did not last long. It was like time was pushing this on to me.

"Mrs. Mallca Siyas-Issigna," the nurse called. Atticus patted my leg and we got up with me rolling my eyes.

They took to a small room where only two people could be inside and still feel somewhat comfortable. Atticus waited outside as she took my vitals. I was completely normal, a temperature of 98.2, a pulse of 72, and a blood pressure of 120/80. Afterwards she brought us to a room and we waited. About five minutes of silence went by and a knock came to the door.

"Hi, my name is Dr. Xavierest, what seems to be the problem today?" he asked coming in shaking our hands.

"Well how should I know? Maybe the one who forced me here can answer your question," I said coldly and glaring at Atticus. I was not happy to be there and he knew it. The doctor turned and looked at Atticus for the answer.

"Well, she has been acting weird these days. She was playing with her sister last night when she accidently smacked her. Mallca freaked out and then had a terrible nightmare last night that left her scared and in a cold sweat. Also what seems to be case after these 'attacks' is that she's labored breathing," he explained. It was not like we all had nightmares and Alaina just surprised me by hitting me. She is little, what else could I do besides tell her no?

"Have you had these nightmares before last night?" Dr. Xavierest asked. I had almost lied to him, but Atticus would have just thrown me under the bus.

"Yes . . ." I confessed.

"How long ago would you say?"

"About a month or so ago," I answered. The doctor wrote down all my answers or any other information I or Atticus had given. We also gave my medical records and other information needed such that involved my time at Prison17-70, both times. It then started to worry me that something was indeed wrong with me.

"Well, I think I am going to have a psychiatrist come in and evaluate you," he answered. The fact that a psychiatrist was needed was a problem and I thought that should be fun letting a man pick and prod at me. "I would like a second pair eyes in the matter."

"About how long will it take?" I asked, "I have to be home at three to meet my sister home and I can't leave her there by herself because she is only four."

"I understand, it should not be too long," he said about to leave.

"Hey, can I speak with you outside?" Atticus piped up.

"Certainly," he replied as the men stepped out of the room away from my listening ear. I had wondered what Atticus had to talk about, but I had the idea it was about me. "What is it you needed to ask me?"

"What do you think she has?" he asked. "I can tell instead of a second pair of eyes you want a second opinion to confirm your suspicions." Doctor Xavierest knew that Atticus had him cornered.

He was not going to be able to leave without telling my worried husband.

He sighed and answered, "I think your wife has PTSD, post-traumatic stress disorder, but a mild case, not like the major ones."

Atticus was speechless as the doctor left to grab the psychiatrist.

He had heard of it before when he was forced to study the disorders in school. He had seen what it does to people with it, but it is different when someone close to you has it. The chances of so much that could actually end up happening increases. Before he came back inside back inside the room he composed himself.

"What did you need to talk to him about?" I asked. Lucky for him a knock came to the door before he had to answer.

"Hello, I'm Dr. Evans. All I am going to do is ask you some questions. I understand that you have been to Prison17-70 twice?" he asked sitting down in the chair. That guy wasted no time jumping right in.

"Yes."

"Any certain treatment?" he asked lightly. I knew what he meant; he was trying to be subtle. He asked if I had any torture. I wished he didn't beat around the bush and come right out.

"I would say too much to my likings."

"Alright, had any major deaths in your family?"

"Yes, there were four and almost myself twice. The four people were my mother, father, brother, and sister-in-law."

"I also see in your profile you have had some other dilemmas," he said. I only nodded in response as he knew that I had technically killed a man.

"I think I have all I need to conclude and agree with Dr.

Xavierest that you may have PTSD," he explained.

My heart had dropped. I understand how that could have happened, but I was strong. I guess that I should have known one day it would catch up to me, but I never imagined like this.

"We can work with this and possible a few medications to help it be easier so you can live a perfectly normal life. Also, even without our help you are still able to, the choice is yours," he explained. I decided to have their help. "You two do not have to worry if you decide to have children because it is not a transfer through genes, but I am sure a few bumps will be along the way."

It was okay, because I didn't want kids.

We left the office at two and arrived home around two-thirty.

I was quiet the entire time as I was trying to soak up all that had just happened in that last two hours. Also having a conversation with Atticus was not on Mallca's to do list anyway. Every once in a while I would glance at him and he would return it. In his looks at me I could perfectly see that his feelings for me had not changed.

In his mind I could see he was thinking about something. I was not going to ask him about until he was the one to bring it up.

"Did you ever think about having kids of our own?" he asked during one of the silent moments as we waited for Alaina to arrive home.

"No," I answered honestly.

"I have. You are so good with Alaina and now that the Predetermine is over it is possible. I think you'd be great," he put out. I never answered him because the door opened with Alaina running in.

"Hi," she greeted coming directly to the chair I had curled myself in. Alaina is a smart girl and saw I did not want to be bothered until I wanted her. She hugged me before running up stairs into her room.

I had so much on my plate with having PTSD and kids had seemed to be a bother. Also it was as I was raising Alaina and keeping Kamva in line anyway. Yes, the dog from Illingsworth's house came to live with us because Alaina could not let the poor thing go to an animal shelter. She said that he was a part of her and she would never let me take it away. I understood and eventually the little rat…dog, grew on me. Well as I thought about it seemed like kids would not be a bad idea. It was not that I did not like them anymore, it was just I'm not really sure. I was afraid of their lives. I told Atticus I would think about it that night that we would see about them when we got older.

Years passed and I learned how to deal with my disorder and the doctor was right about living a normal life. There were some bumps in the road, including bruises, but I turned out alright with help of the ones around me. We explained to Alaina as best we could what was going on and she understood. I was worried that my disorder would ruin my relationship with Atticus, but it actually made us stronger.

About six or so years later I found myself on the porch the same way in my dream. I was twenty-fouryears old and Alaina was now ten getting off the bus. The dream was coming true, but there was one major added detail. Now I was sure the man that was standing behind me was Atticus as he wrapped around me placing his hands on my stomach.

"She is so much like her mother . . . and sister," Atticus said to me nuzzling in my neck.

"Yes she is," I answered leaning my head in.

"You have been so good to her . . . and you'll be great to ours," he said wrapping his fingers and rubbing with thumbs against my bump. Yes, he got me pregnant, twice actually. I decided when I was twenty that kids was a good idea as Alaina was going to grow up and it was safer. I found out I was scared what they would think of me as their mother. Our first child being a boy who we named him Chase and who I was pregnant with at this time. The second was a girl with the name of Irene which is prounouced I-ray-na. That was Atticus's grandmother's name and Chase is my favorite boy name. He likes his mom while Irene likes Atticus a little more than me.

"Atticus . . ." I said looking up into his eyes.

"Mallca . . ." he replied looking down into my eyes.

"I'm kind of scared for us and the little one," I said joining his hand on our baby.

"Don't be, I will always be right beside you."

Like I have said I should thank the Predetermine for the life I have now even though it took some of the most important people away from me. I know I won't forget it. I have a loving husband, a sister, and soon a child of my own in just four months. Still, life is what I, you, decide so make it count.

I stood on my tippy toes toward my soul mate and kissed him. I then said, "I love you and I'm glad you're here with me At least you were always decided."

Alternate Ending

Atticus felt a type sixth sense or partner telepathy that basically told something was wrong ever since the Predetermine ended. Every day that we had been apart he feared for my safety. I was his only true love and he did not know what he could do without me in his life. He had a reason to think that as he had lost his whole world and he did not even know it.

I am not sure, or have any idea on why it happened. All I know is that it was very painful and then it all disappeared. I do not remember much except it was my fifth day back at Prison 17-70 and of course the events were not in my favor. I tried being a good girl and keep my nose out of trouble, but it seems trouble knows how to find me without help required. Batson had beaten me twice that day and it was not even over yet. My lip was busted open and blood still freely ran from it. It was not very much, but I could still feel it. Also, on top of the lip, some bruising in multiple places had begun to appear on my body. By the color of the bruises you

184

could tell what day I received them. The darker was younger and the lighter were older. No one really could tell as they were beaten on again the next day. The most visible one was on the left side of my forehead and it came with a nasty goose bump. It seemed like Batson knew that the end of his days were coming and so he had to get in all the beating on me while he was able to. However, that day was one I decided I had enough and fought back.

He had just slapped me once again, for absolutely nothing, and I decided to sock him in the nose instead of the jaw this time. With me being older this time I had some extra power behind my punch resulting in a broken nose. Also having physical education helped in the power department. Still, when I hit him again it almost felt more rewarding than the first time. As before he stood up and fixed his crooked nose before striking back. Not to mention the only injury I received was the busted lip. My lip was the least of my worries.

"Mallca," I heard my name while sitting in the barrack during the break period the guards are ordered to give us. I learned that his name was Jack, "Some of us can't wait anymore for this to end so we're making a break for it tonight. Are you in?"

The last time that happened I remember that someone I love dearly died. I will not go through that again and it could one of my friends or my own life this time. With all that I left back in civilization I was not going to be stupid and make a break for it. That could be just what they want and I wasn't going to lose my family or make us all pay a price. They were all I had left and I learned from my mistakes.

"No, and you all should give it some time," I reasoned. No one else needed to die for these silly reasons. I could just sense that if I hung in a little longer it would all pay off.

"I'm sorry, but I am finished waiting around while they plan on how to kill us before we are allowed to leave," Jack said leaving and returning to the group of want to be fugitives. I figured this escape would happen tonight by the way they were all gathered together. All I did then was lie down on my cot and wait it out. For me it was easier to wait instead of risk my life. Night came quickly and before I knew it, it was all over.

I ended up falling asleep and the sound that awoke me that was not people's movements, but the cracks of gunfire. I jumped up with a fright and my heart immediately started pounding. It sounded exactly like the night Vaughan was killed except it was not as loud because I was inside and not out there with them. I wondered how long it would last. About after two minutes all the noises stopped and all was in a silence. That only meant one thing: all the people involved were dead just like the last time. The guards make sure that everyone who tried to escape was dead to make an example for the smart ones who decided to stay out of the mess. I was actually curious about what had happened out there and wondered if anyone survived. If they were nearby may be, just may be, I could help them out. I felt it was repaying what happened to Vaughan by saving another person's life. Slowly I opened the barrack door and it creaked from the rusty hinges. I saw that I was too late. Everyone on the ground was dead. I was glad I did not join them. However, what had happened next was what I never thought would happen for a long time.

I heard one last crack of gunfire and jumped at the sound. I did not know where it came from or its intended target. The one piece of information I knew about the gunfire was where the bullet had landed. A gut wrenching pain and wet sensation came to my body covering every nerve. I slowly looked down and wished I hadn't. The bullet implanted itself right in my stomach of all places. All my strength was drained as I toppled over falling outside the door. Everything was going black, but I heard three faint voices.

"She finally got what the little bitch deserved," I heard in slurred drunken manner and I knew that it was Batson. He was the one who had shot me. He finally got the last fight and he won, but I have my own back-up.

"I knew you were a bastard. She had done nothing!" Maurus screamed drawing his weapon and aiming it Batson. Before Batson could react with his own Maurus fired a kill shot right through where his heart was supposed to be. He died instantly and I got the fight and the revenge.

"Oh no Mallca! Will she be alright?" Rimdara asked as Maurus was trying to get me to an empty cot. He then applied pressure and I was not aware of anything around me, but I just wanted the pain to stop. I weakly tried to push him away. From what my blurry eyes could see the blood loss and location of the hit was too great. The bullet had hit some of my major organs.

"I know it hurts, but I need to stop the bleeding," he reasoned. It wasn't going to work on me. I knew what had to be done and I was prepared for my end.

"You'll be alright sweetie," Rimdara cooed. I didn't believe her; I believed I was going to die.

"No," I whispered, "Will one of you tell my family I . . . love them and not to burden my loss."

"I won't have to because you're going to see them tomorrow. I got word minutes ago that we are to release all of you," Maurus informed trying to give me hope, to give strength and the will to survive.

"Please . . ." I pleaded in a raspy voice. I had to hear that someone would make they got the message or I didn't know what I'd do.

"I will," Rimdara agreed to my last wish as she started to sob.

Even though I had not known Rimdara very long I considered her a friend. Maurus was already my friend and I knew he was not going to let me die without a fight after all we have been through.

Everything began to grow darker and lighter all at the same time, but also colder. My breaths became slower and harder to follow through. I could hear so many voices of both the living plane and spiritual. My family was waiting on the other side. My eyes fluttered as I grew weaker and weaker by the second. The seconds left of my life followed. My headed tilted and lost all focus. When all my strength had dissipated, when I could no longer hold on, I, the wyvern, Mallca, had died.

I was right when I said they should have waited. I did hear when Maurus told me that the next morning we would be released.

It all ended the next day and I mean all of the Predetermine's ways and all after the day I died. I always wanted to help and be the hero, even in this case I'm the tragic hero.

Atticus and Alaina came to the first entrance gate of Prison 17-70. They were both excited to see me again, but to Atticus nothing felt right. However, since I had died only the night before the call had not been made informing them of the tragic news. Seeing the rest of the joyous people with their love ones made waiting less bearable.

Finally he could not wait any longer so he grabbed Alaina's hand and went searching for me. It was not me he saw, but another familiar face.

"Maurus," Atticus said walking up.

"Atticus . . ." Maurus replied tensing up at the sight of him.

"Maurus, is this Atticus?" Rimdara said as she stood with him.

"Mommy!" they all heard a little boy that ran into Rimdara arms. Rimdara grabbed a young boy about Alaina's age and wrapped him in her arms as tight as she could. She nuzzled into his face as the boy tried to push her away. She couldn't let him go, not yet, she wasn't going to until she was sure she wasn't going to lose him again.

"Yes, this Mallca's husband and her little sister Alaina," Maurus explained to Rimdara. Upon hearing my name being brought up Atticus wondered where I was. However, the others had tears welling up in their eyes.

"Speaking of Mallca, where is she?" he asked. The two looked at each other wondering who should break the news. It was finally Maurus.

"Atticus, I'm sorry. Mallca's dead."

Atticus was not sure what he just heard out of Maurus's mouth.

Was this some kind of a sick joke and I was going to appear out of nowhere and surprise him. If it was, it was not funny to Atticus and it would never be. By the facial expressions of the people around him Atticus could see no one was not pulling a prank.

"How did it happen? When did it happen?" Atticus asked spitting out anything that came to his mind. Alaina was not sure what was going on, but something was wrong. She heard my name and Atticus was upset.

"Last night, there was an attempted breakout. Mallca had nothing to do with it, but she opened the barrack door and Batson shot her," he explained.

"One . . . more . . . day," Atticus muttered under his breath trying to fight the tears that he wasn't ready to shed.

"I did everything I could to save her."

"You mean all you could without being caught!" Atticus snapped coming out of his moment of shock. Atticus's temper usually does sometimes get the best of him and it was worse because he just lost the one he loves. There would be no happy reunion for us, just a funeral.

"No, I made sure that bastard would never hurt another soul again!" Maurus exclaimed making Atticus knew no one got away with this.

"Batson's dead?" Atticus quickly and quietly asked returning to a controlled state.

All Maurus did was nod.

"The last thing she said was for me to tell you that she loved you and Alaina and wanted you to move on and know she'll be with you," Rimdara told him adding the last part that I did not say, but was true.

Atticus knew that I would be the person to say that to them in my time of dying. I would not want him to sit around the rest of their beautiful free lives mourning my death. Alaina is too young for that and Atticus had a new start to begin. Alaina may not understand it quite yet what happened to her family, but I knew Atticus would take care of her. He got back up on his feet after Bethany and Daphnia, but I know it will be just as challenging with me. I just know they will and did turn out alright.

Alaina

At first I did not understand what happened to either my family or my older sister Mallca. Later I came to know that they had died. Atticus only told me that they had gone away and I will see them all again one day. Of course I asked many questions and he said that it was okay they were gone because they were not in anymore pain and in a better place. It was not until I turned eight I knew what he meant by that. I still miss her as for some time she was my whole world. She did everything to save me and give me a better place to live. I miss all my family even though I only knew some of them for a short time or never even met. At least I still had Atticus and a woman I knew as Rimdara to lean on. They helped me when times got rough, but Atticus was always there.

Rimdara's son, Mitchel, actually became one of my best friends as we were always close together when we were little. Since Rimdara was usually over to help I saw him about every day and we just clicked. We were like the new Mallca and Atticus on the block. Our guardian and parent tried to see of they could separate us, but I couldn't be away from Mitchy. He hates that nickname, but I think it is cute plus he usually picks on me so it is only fair I get to embarrass him.

Anyway, I remember Atticus telling me stories of him and Mallca at night or anytime I asked. They were all different types, from sad to funny. They were excellent bedtime stories. I think it gave him both closure and remembrance. Afterward I'd see a few tears in his eyes, but I'd just hug and he'd be fine. However, I thought it was mean when Atticus later joked with me about it could be a repeat of him and Mallca, but with me and Mitchel. I thought yah right.

Well, I was proven wrong in my junior year of high school when Mitchel Zarcovsky asked me to prom after my boyfriend had broken up with me to take the trash queen. Afterwards of that night, I kissed him and we began dating. I felt like my sister and fell for my best friend. Atticus told me that was who your soul mate should be, your best friend.

Everyone says my generation is a lucky one because it was when the Predetermine ended and we do not have to go through it. I always thought it was the twelve and thirteen year olds who had yet to receive theirs were lucky, but I guess it can sway either direction. Speaking of the Predetermine, it actually gave me a title. To some people I was known as Illingsworth's daughter or step-daughter, while to the others I was Mallca's baby sister. However, I think my favorite one is Daughter of the Breaking. Mitchel gave me that one. I tell them only one of those titles is actually true. That man had no right in what he did to me...or Mallca.

I grew up being what I wanted to be and it can be told by my love for animals. I became a veterinarian and loved every minute of the job except when I lost one. I married my high school sweetheart and best friend Mitchel. Rimdara was trilled and said she always knew that it would happen the first time she saw me. Like Mallca did when she married Atticus keeping her last name and added his on the end with a hyphen. He understood my reason because the Siyas family needed to be remembered. I became Alaina Kenari Siyas-Zarcovsky. A year later I had my first child and like my mother the gender was female. Mitchel agreed to the name I picked out for her and everyone thought it was a perfect fit to a beautiful girl, Mallca Chay Siyas-Zarcovsky.

Atticus

After being informed of Mallca's death and I snapped on Maurus I had broken down. Rimdara's words did not reach me all the way through the first time. I did shut myself out and Alaina seemed to be on her own at five. Then her words struck harder at me as if Mallca had slapped in the back of the head and I understood. It was like when Bethany and my mother died, who I still miss as much as Mallca. I knew Mallca did not want me to do this and forget about who needed me. I could not do that to

Alaina or myself. So I just picked myself up again and started the new chapter she had given her life to give me. I knew she loved me.

When Alaina went to school so did I. I went to college to begin my dream job, working with history as an archeologist. I actually did a report, wrote a few papers, and a novel on the Predetermine that went to the best sellers. I was known as an expert on the matter and it partly because I had experienced it firsthand. I finished schooling just when Alaina was about to enter junior high school. Afterwards I did work around home until Alaina finished high school. I did tell her that she would end up with Mitchel, but she did not listen to me. She is so like her mother and sister. As a child she would say it was gross...I see that is not the way now. When she finished college and was out on her own I traveled. I had this feeling that Mallca went with me. She said she hated history, but what she really hated was learning about dates and people that did not interest her, not the concept itself. She also loved to explore and travel. She would have made a great partner in this field with me.

The question became a complete surprise to me when Alaina asked me to walk her down the aisle at her wedding. I said I would as long as she answered one question. My question to her was... why? She said I was like a father to her even though I am her brother-in-law. I was touched by what she said and actually cried. I cried again seeing her in the beautiful white dress I found in a collection of the Issigna family. Like Mallca did with the graduation dress, Alaina first turned it down until we talked about it. She then accepted it and thanked me for all I had done for her. I was honored when the wedding day finally arrived. I still wish Mallca and I could have had one, but at least I got to marry the girl of my dreams before she was ripped away. Some people don't get that chance.

When Mallca Chay was born a year later I was touched and cried again at the happiness it brought to me. Alaina named her daughter after her sister and it was a perfect idea. I think Mallca would be embarrassed and touched by the action of her sister. I could see her knowing this information and having a face bright as a cherry. Something she always got embarrassed about was when someone talked about her in up lifting ways. It was the cutest look and much better than the glare. I miss that too, but I don't want her to know that.

I did everything I believed Mallca would have wanted me to do if she was here to tell me herself. I moved on and took care of Alaina. Alaina grew up to a smart and successful young lady. I never remarried, but I tired dating a couple times. I never worked out as I am still in love and married to Mallca. I know I'm widower, but it is not the same. I knew she probably wanted me to revisit love, but she was the only person I could ever transmit that feeling to. I just couldn't do it as each girl reminded me of her. It doesn't matter as I still moved on with Mallca by my side. I, Atticus Issigna, will always know and be sure of that the Predetermine will never control us again and I love Mallca Siyas who is the girl who gave her life so the real life could be revealed.

Printed in the United States
By Bookmasters